This book is dedicated to my mother and father
Moyra and Alan Davies.

Colin Davies

was born in Brighton in 1970. He started his school life at Downs Infants before moving to Hollingbury in 1976 where he went to Carden. After moving up to the junior school Colin started writing stories. His work was recognised by his teachers and during this time had a number of short stories published in the school magazine.

After attending Patcham Fawcett High School Colin continued his studies at Brighton Technical College delving into the world of computers, this didn't last very long as in 1988 he moved to Blackpool. It was while he was working as a salesman in the Hi-Fi industry that Colin made the decision to start writing more seriously. Influences by Lewis Carol, Douglas Adams and Roald Dahl Colin embarked on his journey into Children's literature, and so far, his having a really fun time.

D1372572

Cover Design by Mark 'George' Stephenson

Illustrations by Lindsey Boon

First Published by Ivory Moon Limited (7 Aug 2006)

ISBN-10: 1905949006

ISBN-13: 978-1905949007

Kindle Edition Published by Colin Davies (26 Aug 2010)

This Edition Published Via Lulu.com

ISBN-13: 978-1-4716-2205-2

Mathamagical

by

Colin Davies

Acknowledgments and Big Thanks

First and foremost I have to send out a big thank you and acknowledge to the inspiration of Jennifer Ireland. At the age of 13 she had to write a synopsis for a nonsense story as part of her homework. At that time I was her personal tutor helping her with Computer Studies, Mathematics and English. Jennifer already had the idea of a small boy and a talking snake. I said she should call the snake Adder and send the boy on an 'Alice in Wonderland' styled journey in a world of maths. After this discussion I thought this was too good to be left as a school project. Jennifer told me to write the book, so I did. Even though much has changed, as a notice of recognition I have kept the boys name, Adder and a couple of other character names. Thanks so much Jen.

Next I would like to give love and thanks to my fiancée Heather Brennan. She has had to put up with me talking about this magical land for far too long. Heather's belief in this book has been both a drive and inspiration.

A big thanks goes to both Tony McMullen and Paula Currey for all their help. Their comments during the initial proofreading process have been invaluable.

Heather's mother Patricia has been wonderfully encouraging and I could not write this section without saying thank you.

My passion for mathematics was something that was encouraged through my childhood by my mother Moyra Davies. It was with great pride when I presented her with a copy of this book. I can say without doubt that if it wasn't for my mother's influence in my education, and the love and support she has given me over the years, this book could not have existed.

I can also say the same for my father Alan Davies. It was the worst day of my life when he died in 2001. Where my mother gave me my mathematic abilities, it was my father who encouraged my imagination. Both me and my brother Raymond owe a grate debt to both our parents for the way they raised us. Without them we could not have achieved any of the things we have in our lives.

Much respect and gratitude goes to Janette Calverley of Ivory Moon for all the work she has put into this project. She has believed in me since she first read the synopsis and has been instrumental in getting this story into print. I also need to thank Barbara Wilkie, my friend, proofreader and agent, with a massive thanks going out to her husband Derek and daughter Rebecca for the kind words and advice.

Last but by no mean least I would like to thank all my friends: Mick Arthur, Iayn Dobsyn, Chris Giles, Dylan Freeman, Jason and Annie Brachial, Matthew Bartlett and Chris Wright. These people have always believed in my ability to write and have encouraged me at every turn.

If I have forgotten anyone, I'm very sorry, you know I love you.

1x1=1

2x1=2

3x1=3

4x1=4

5x1=5

6x1=6

7x1=7

8x1=8

9x1=9

10x1=10

Chapter

1

one

Chapter One

"It's not fair," Ben sobbed sitting on the edge of his bed. His Harry Potter and Lord of the Rings posters gazed down at him, "I didn't cheat!"

Ben held his breath in a feeble attempt to stop crying. His face turned a beetroot colour and, despite his best efforts, the tears flowed as soon as he started to draw in the air again. He was so upset about what had happened that he couldn't think straight. Why did mum and Stephen, his stepfather, always believe his teachers rather than him?

"It's just not fair."

He kicked the football lying on the floor in front of his bed. The ball shot across the room, ricocheted off his wardrobe and leapt up onto the shelf where he kept all his toy figures. With a crash, the ball careered through his collection of plastic Middle Earth monsters, knocking them flying in every direction.

This was more than Ben could bear. He threw himself face down on his bed and wept uncontrollably into his pillow. The wind and rain were getting stronger outside and it was obvious that the storm had set in for the night.

It had started to rain around two o'clock in the afternoon, about the time Ben had been called to the headmasters' office. It was quite embarrassing to be summoned in the middle of a lesson. Tracy Spinkle had entered his double geography period holding a folded piece of paper and handed it to Mr Turnpike who duly opened it up and read its contents in his usual deep monotone.

"Ben Small, can you please go to the headmaster's office?"

Ben's palms started sweating, he knew it was trouble. He ran his fingers through his blond hair, stood up, straightened his blue school blazer and with his head down solemnly, left the room.

He walked through the corridors of Cottomwall Grammar without taking any notice of anyone or anything. His mind was racing, trying to figure out what on earth he had done wrong now. Somehow he had acquired a reputation for mischief. If anything untoward happened, his was the first name out of the hat.

The headmaster's office, with its wall of leather bound books and heavy rosewood furniture all finished with green leather, reminded Ben of the local library. It was an old building filled with dark wood. Even the decoration was the same, cream wallpaper with gold feathers forming the pattern, though in the headmaster's office it looked like it had been hung upside down.

Ben's heart sank when he saw his parents sat across from Mr Granville; this was big trouble! He recognised the pile of papers on the large solid desk that separated his parents from the headmaster. It was the English test Ben and his classmates had taken last week to calculate their progress. They seemed to be tested all the time in one subject or another. Ben had felt very good about the English paper. It was one of his favourite subjects and this had been the first time they had been tested on English since moving up from juniors.

Mr Granville gestured Ben to sit down next to his mother. Both his parents looked angry. Stephen watched as Ben took his seat then, shaking his head, turned his attention back to the headmaster.

"Cheating," began the white-haired ex general, "will not be tolerated in this school."

"Cheating?" questioned Ben. He may not listen in class and is prone to playing the odd practical joke but cheating! "I never…"

"I have here the results from your English test last week," the headmaster held up a piece of paper, "and it makes interesting reading." He perched his small wire framed spectacles that looked like the top half of the lens had been cut off, on the end of his nose. "97%"

Ben smiled and looked up at his mum, for some reason she didn't seem pleased. He looked back at Mr Granville. The most disapproving glare Ben had ever seen emanated over the top of Mr Granville's half glasses and headed straight in his direction.

Ben was shocked. "You think I cheated?"

Granville leaned forward, "Are you denying it?"

∞

"Yes I am!"

The head opened one of the drawers in his desk, removed another pile of papers and tapped them on the desktop to make sure they were straight before he flicked through them.

"In the other subjects you've been tested on your scores are very average." He started dealing each piece of paper onto the desk reading from them as he did so, "Geography Average, Science Average, History is above average but your maths is well below standard. This English result is so out of character with the rest of your scores that it leaves us with only one conclusion."

"But I'm good at English!" Ben's defence fell on deaf ears.

"You're in enough trouble," Stephen sounded furious, "don't make it worse by lying."

Ben could feel the frustration build up inside him. Not only had he been wrongly accused but he'd been tried, judged and sentenced without any defence. This was how it always happened. At parents evening the teachers would tell them what Ben had been up to and without any chance of defending his actions they'd take the side of his teachers and he'd be punished. This time their reluctance to believe his innocence mortified Ben. He'd never cheated at anything in his life. Not even while playing card games with his Gran and that would be easy.

She was very old now and wasn't really sure of the rules anymore. She would have believed him, but no one except Ben would listen to what she had to say anymore. Ben loved visiting his Gran in Manchester, he felt they didn't make the 300-mile trip up north often enough. She had so many wonderful stories about strange lands and talking animals. It was listening to his Gran telling her stories that got Ben interested in English.

Now, lying on his bed, branded a cheat, suspended from school for a week and grounded with no television or comics for a month, Ben decided he couldn't go on. He couldn't put up with never being believed. It was time to leave, time to run away.

He started to gather his belongings. First, he retrieved his rucksack from under a pile of old board games and comic book annuals at the bottom of his wardrobe. He'd put it there with the best intentions of using it again after returning home from a wonderful weekend in the woods with Stephen and two of his mates from school, John Baxter and Simon Duffy.

His stepfather had bought him a tent for his 10th birthday and had taken them to Grumpton Forest. A huge expanse of woodland with well kept hiking paths running through it. Ben had been up there several times with Stephen but had never spent a night under the stars.

His mum wasn't one for the great outdoors so she used to stay at home. Ben never knew what his mum did while they went on their walks. He imagined that she stayed in spending all her time cooking so when they returned there would always have a fantastic stew with big stodgy dumplings. The stew was even more fantastic and the dumpling even more stodgy and delicious when they came back from their camping adventure. That was just over a year ago. Ben smiled at the memory, then, remembering why he'd got his rucksack out again, frowned. All the stew and dumplings in the world couldn't stop him.

He rummaged through his drawers.
"I need socks," he said to himself, being careful not to speak to loud in case he was overheard, "and underpants."

He took the underwear out and placed it on his bed counting them as he put them down. Twelve pairs of socks, three odd coloured socks and ten pairs of underpants, "that should do."

He tried picking them all up at once. A couple of the rolled up pairs of socks and one of the odd ones fell to the floor. He pushed what he held onto into his rucksack. A pair of his underpants escaped but fearing the floor they clung onto the side of his Bart Simpson bedspread. Ben grabbed the loose garments and reunited them with the others in his luggage.
"T-shirts and trousers."

He opened the next drawer down. His mother had folded all his T-shirts and placed them so that the picture on the front was face up. Ben scanned the gallery of cartoon characters and rock bands. There on the left was the one shirt he couldn't be without, his Manchester City top. That had to come with him. He carefully packed it then returned to the drawer. He knew he didn't have the room for all of them, trousers, toiletries and some books had to go in yet.

"Oh and jumpers."

He picked out some at random and stuffed them in. His trousers were hanging in the wardrobe, nothing smart he thought.

He grabbed two pairs of jog pants and a pair of tracksuit bottoms, the school trousers he was wearing would do for the first leg of his journey.

He collected a couple of fleeces from the drawer under his bed and pushed them on top of the jog pants. Next he turned his attention to the bookshelf. Knowing he couldn't take his Playstation he decided to take a couple of his favourite books; but what to choose? Ben liked reading and his collection had become quite comprehensive. He moved the index finger of his left-hand back and forth over the spines stopping every so often to think about the title.

"Harry Potter? Which one?" He placed his right index finger on his lower lip to help him think, "Chamber of Secrets."

He took the book out and placed it on top of the drawers then continued his search.

"Ah, Alice in Wonderland," this had always been one of his best books. He must have read it twenty times, "can't go without you."

He put it on top of Harry and looked back at the shelf.

"One more will do?"

He continued to search in the same way as before but this time thinking even harder. Action or fantasy? Scary or science fiction? He was caught between the Hobbit, one of his Goosebumps collection, an H G Wells or a book about the making of Star Wars.

"Well I am going on a journey?" he pondered over The Hobbit, "and I will be on my own." He crossed the Goosebumps off his mental list. He didn't want anything to scare him while he was out on his own. Holding that thought he crossed off the H G Wells Books, "I like them, but too scary for this trip."

The making of Star Wars was a big hard-backed book. Ben picked it up and flicked through the pages. He closed the book and lifted it up and down to check the weight.

"Too heavy." He slotted the movie book back on the shelf and removed The Hobbit from its normal home. "As my Gran likes to say 'you should always go with your first choice'"

He gathered the books together and walked back to his bed. Two of the books were packed in the main storage area of the rucksack and one in the side pocket for easy access.

"I'll start with you Alice." He told the book as he slipped it into the pocket with a small pen torch in case it was dark on the train. "Now for the toiletries..."

Slowly opening his bedroom door Ben peered through the gap to see if anybody was there. The hallway was empty. He could hear the sound of the TV in the distance. Ben stepped out of his room. A sudden noise from the lower floor halted his progress, quickened his breathing and nearly pushed his heart into his throat. His mum and Stephen were laughing hard at the programme they were watching, so Ben was now sure that both his parents were downstairs.

Pretending to be James Bond, Ben crept towards the bathroom. With his back to the door he opened it and silently slipped in.

Toothpaste, toothbrush, flannel, a couple of towels and some soap, that should do it? He took the old supermarket plastic bag that was used as a makeshift bin liner out of the bronze coloured metal dustbin. There were only a couple of cotton wool buds that his mum had used to remove her make-up in there so he dropped them into the empty bin and put his toiletries in the bag.

Tucking the bag under his arm, he prepared himself for the return journey to his bedroom. He slowly opened the door, looking to the right, nothing, left. His heart stopped for a moment. He could see from the shadow on the wall that someone was coming up the stairs. Ben quickly shut the door and locked it. With his ear to the door he could hear the mysterious shadow

∞

walking down the hallway. The door handle suddenly rattled, Ben jumped back. Stephen's voice came through the door.

"Is that you in there Ben?"

Ben looked around for somewhere to hide but it was pointless. His stepfather obviously knew it was Ben as his mother was still downstairs.

"Yes." He replied flushing the toilet.

"Well remember to wash your hands."

He ran the tap to give himself time to think. There was no way out of it, Stephen was waiting outside the door and Ben had to get past him with his bag of toiletries. He scrunched the bag up as tight as he could but it was no use, the towels were too bulky.

"I'll have to leave them," he whispered.

Taking the towels out of the bag he replaced them on the towel rack. Now the bag would wrap tight enough the shove down his trousers. He pushed it down the front but it was still too bulky. He looked like a boy with a plastic bag full of toiletries shoved down the front of his trousers. BANG! BANG! BANG!

"Come on Ben, What are you doing in there?"

Ben's dressing gown twitched on the back of the door as it shook with the knocking.

That's it, he thought, my dressing gown.

Ben hurriedly grabbed the dressing gown and wrestled it on. It was hard to get your arms into towelling sleeves when you're rushing. It was slightly twisted but he managed it. He wrapped the gown around himself and tied the towel belt. Now you couldn't tell he was hiding something.

He turned off the tap and unlocked the door. Sheepishly he left the bathroom. Stephen was looking at him with a stern face.

"What have you been doing?" He snapped, "you'd better not have made a mess."

Ben shook his head in reply and wandered back to his room. After shutting the door he took in a deep breath.

"That was close."

∞

He packed the toilet bag in his rucksack and sat on the bed next to it. The rain was hitting the window hard now and Ben started to have second thoughts.

"Where am I going to go?" he asked himself.

The cheating allegation and his overwhelming feeling of injustice filled Ben's thoughts again. He couldn't see things changing around here and, in his mind, running away was the only solution. All this fussing around had clouded his judgement and despite the foul weather it seemed like the right thing to do.

He put on his raincoat and zipped it up tight. Looking out of the window he could see the trees moving in the wind. The driving rain looked solid in the streetlights and Ben had to count to ten in his head before opening the window.

That was a trick his Gran had taught him some years ago, "If you're not sure if you're doing the right thing," she'd say, "close your eyes and count to ten. If you still think it's right then do it."

"That's it!" Ben now knew where he was going. He'd go and visit his Gran. He wasn't sure how much a train ticket to Manchester would cost, but he was sure he had enough to get there.

He also realised that the one thing he had forgotten was money. He took down the washed out syrup tin he used to keep his birthday money in and opened it. Three ten pound notes, a fiver and some loose change. Ben added it up in his head, £35 plus change. That should get him there. He pushed the money into his trouser pocket and returned to the window.

A deep breath to steady his nerves then, woooosh! Without the window to stop them, the wind and rain forcefully entered Ben's bedroom. Ben stepped back in surprise, his face soaked by the elements.

"No turning back now," he said to motivate himself and with that he climbed out of the window.

Ben had climbed out of this window on several occasions but never in weather like this. About one metre below the windowsill was the flat roof of the garage. Ben dropped his rucksack out first then slowly lowered himself down. He was tall enough to reach back up and close the window. Next was the longer drop to the garden. The wind threw the rain against him with some force but Ben was determined. Again his backpack went first; he scrambled over the edge of the roof and allowed himself to hang by his finger tips. Once he felt steady he let go and dropped softly to the ground.

The side of the garage was sheltered from the wind which made it easy for Ben to strap on his rucksack. The night was cold and Ben was already soaked to the skin. Using the bushes as cover to hide from the windows in case his parents were looking out, he made his way to the road. The weather was keeping people indoors so Lightridge Avenue was deserted.

The walk to Cottomwall train station was three kilometres and the route would take him past his school. Head down, shoulders hunched and hands in pockets, Ben started his journey. Unlike Bilbo Baggins in The Hobbit, Ben didn't have a party of dwarves to catch up with or a grey haired old wizard to give him comforting words when he caught up with them. He felt something in his pocket.

"I've even got my handkerchief," he said smiling.

Ben had been walking against the wind for about twenty minutes when he realised he had reached the school gates. The weather had been getting progressively worse during this time and Ben was very cold and tired. He stopped to look at the main doors; there was light coming through them. Was the door open? Slowly he entered through the gates to have a closer look. The light was definitely coming through an open door.
The caretaker must be working late tonight? He thought.

He knew there wasn't a parents evening tonight, and the rehearsals for the school play didn't start for another two weeks. This year they were performing Alice in Wonderland.

Ben had auditioned for the part of the frog footman. It wasn't a big part but Ben knew the scene so well being as it was one of his favourite books. He desperately wanted to be part of it and was bitterly disappointed when he didn't even get a stagehand job.

The cold caused him to shiver and he thought about the wait at the train station.

"Maybe I could camp in the school for the night?"

This seemed like a great idea. He was cold and tired and stopping the night in the school meant he could dry off and, as long as he set off for the station early enough, he could be gone before anyone knew he was there. Back in James Bond mode, Ben sneaked up to the door. The coast was clear so, moving very quietly, he entered.

The corridors of the school seemed larger and longer than they did during the day when they were filled with people going about their daily school business. He could feel the emptiness of the school. He had walked down these hallways many a time without anyone else around, but knowing that the classrooms were abandoned seemed to add an echo and loneliness to the building. Ben headed for the science rooms.

They had a snake living in a glass tank there and Ben remembered Mr Trot, the science teacher, telling them that the room had to be kept warm for it. He also knew where Mr Trot hid the key. For a teacher he had a very bad memory. So as too not lose the key he balanced it on top of the doorframe. He never told anybody, Ben saw him put it there one day.

There always seemed to be a broken chair in the corridor outside the science room. Ben started to pull it across to the door so he could reach the key. The scraping noise it made on the smooth, polished floor stopped Ben after only a couple of centimetres. A moment of stillness passed as he listened for the footsteps of someone coming to investigate the teeth-jarring screech, nothing. This time Ben lifted the chair and carried it over to the door. He climbed up and felt along the doorframe. There it was, looking like his front door key but silver.

Click, the door opened. Ben entered, thought about switching the light on then realised that he would only draw attention to himself. He closed and locked the door behind him. It was warm in there yet Ben was still shivering.

He removed his wet jacket and hung it on the back of one of the chairs. He thought he'd have a bit of a read before going to sleep. He pulled his book out of the pocket of his rucksack and found his torch. Tucking himself into a corner under one of the workbenches that were fixed to the wall like one big shelf round the edge of the classroom, he curled up, opened the book at page one and in the light of his torch joined Alice on her adventures. It wasn't long before his eyes began to shut.

He switched off the torch and placed it next to the book on the floor beside him. The sound of the storm made him feel cold. Wrapping his arms around his knees Ben laid his head on his rucksack and fell asleep.

$1 \times 2 = 2$

$2 \times 2 = 4$

$3 \times 2 = 6$

$4 \times 2 = 8$

$5 \times 2 = 10$

$6 \times 2 = 12$

$7 \times 2 = 14$

$8 \times 2 = 16$

$9 \times 2 = 18$

$10 \times 2 = 20$

Chapter

2
two

∞

Chapter Two

The wind pushed hard against the trees in Cottomwall, swaying them this way and that. It was bashing the branches with all its might and forcing them to give up their leaves that had just turned yellow and brown for the autumn.

Even Old Invincible, the old horse chestnut tree, was beginning to feel the power of the storm. He had stood in the grounds of the Grammar School for over 100 years and had been given his name back in World War II. During an air raid one winter's night in 1943, a German Doodlebug crashed into the school building right next to the proud tree. He took the full force of the explosion. The building was wrecked yet somehow the tree stood strong. The only damage he sustained was some scorching on his trunk. From that day on, he became know as Old Invincible.

Now his old branches creaked and cracked in the swirling air. His seasoned trunk, thick with age, resisted the onslaught for as long as it could. The honeycomb of tunnel's made by the ants that had seen the great tree as a suitable home some months before had weakened the solid structure and, against the pressure of the persistent gale, it started to give way. The mighty Old Invincible, who had given conkers to generations, began to creak and crack and crack and creak.

The trunk split, the blustering wind saw the weakness and pushed Old Invincible to the point of no return. Gravity took control and the once proud, tall, woody plant splintered and broke in two. The bottom half, with its roots deep in the ground stood fast, its top careered towards the grammar school buildings.

In a last, desperate, attempt to halt the descent, Old Invincible threw out a branch against the building and, with a crash, it went straight through the window of the science room. His flailing limb scattered glass in every direction. It continued into the room, pushing the venetian blinds against the snake tank which, in turn, slid the reptile's glass home off the bench and onto the floor where it exploded into thousands of shards, throwing its occupant into the far corner of the room.

∞

Ben woke with a start. The smashing glass of both the window and the snake tank had violently interrupted his slumber. It took him a couple of seconds to realise where he was. He recoiled into the corner, scared. The darkness of the room and the noise of the storm invaded his senses and disorientated him. He scrambled around with his hand to find his torch. If he remembered correctly he had placed it down next to his book before falling asleep.

Frantically, he glided his hand around on the floor until he felt something. His fingers investigated the object, paper with a hard spine, that's the book. He moved his fingers feeling around the general area of the novel. His digits felt something hard and cylindrical, he grabbed it. Definitely the torch, he could feel the on/off switch. Just as he was picking it up something moved passed his hand brushing it as it went. Ben snatched his hand into his chest. Shaking with fear he pointed the torch into the dark and switched it on.

The circular light, bright in the middle and dim around the outside but well enough to see, illuminated the room. As Ben moved the torch, odd shadows which seemed to have a life of their own, danced across the floor and walls. He held his breath as he scanned the room. First to his left, chairs, desks, nothing unusual, slowly he swept the light across the empty class. More chairs, more desks, snake. SNAKE!

Staring straight at him was the snake from the tank.
"Hello," said the snake.

Ben screamed and jumped up banging his head hard on the bench above knocking himself unconscious. The torch fell to the floor. Rolling around in a half circle, the lamp ended up pointing into Ben's face as he lay in a crumpled heap.

The noise of the storm was the first thing Ben heard as he came round. He opened his eyes and immediately shut them again. The torchlight was very bright in his face and it hurt his eyes. He reached out a hand to pick up the light. With his eyes shut, he moved himself into an upright sitting position. Taking a deep breath he opened his eyes. The room was still the same, glass

∞

all over the floor on the other side, the weather outside was still encroaching through the broken window and the snake was still in front of him. SNAKE!

Ben controlled himself this time and didn't jump up. He sat perfectly still, his heart trying desperately to free itself from his chest. The snake swayed slightly to the left then back to the right. It looked like it was checking him out. "Are you alright?" it asked sounding very concerned, "You banged your head quite hard."

"You can talk?"

The snake spoke with a slight hiss to his voice so his S's sounded more like the TH sound at the beginning of words like THE and THIS.

"Yeth I can." The snake raised itself up looking very proud, "I am General Adder."

Ben wasn't sure how to react; he'd never met a snake before let alone a talking one. It seemed polite enough so Ben thought he'd better be polite too. "I'm Ben, Ben Small, pleased to meet you."

"Likewise," the General tilted his head, "what are you doing here, if you don't mind me asking?"

"I'm sorry General Adder but I've never met a talking snake before, where do you come from?"

The snake slithered closer.

"I was in that glass tank over there." Using his tail he pointed across the room, "something pushed it off the top and I was freed."

Ben had seen that snake in the tank many times. Most of the time it was asleep and on the odd occasion it wasn't he'd never heard it talk. He had never heard anyone else say they'd heard the snake talking either come to think of it and he told the General this.

"Please, call me Adder," the snake said with a smile. "I have never talked before because I was trapped and there was no point. I have been sent to find someone to help me but being stuck in that glass prison meant I couldn't find the right person."

"Oh," replied Ben, a little embarrassed.

"I've only spoken to you because I didn't expect to find anyone here at this time of night."

"No, you wouldn't."

Ben was curious about what Adder had said. He was looking for someone to help him? As he had asked so many questions of the talking snake Ben decided to tell Adder why he was there. It would be an exchange of information and he wouldn't feel so bad about continuing the inquisition.

"I've run away from home."

"Really, why?"

Ben told him everything. How he'd been wrongly accused of cheating when he hadn't done anything wrong, how his parents believed the headmaster instead of him, how they used the fact that he was no good at maths to prove he couldn't be that good at English.

"And I'm really good at English as well."

Adder smiled, you could almost see him thinking about something.

"I'm sorry for your troubles," he said with genuine sentiment. "I arrived here under completely different circumstances. I was sent here by the Council of Numbers from the land of Mathamagical where I'm the General of the Plus Regiment."

"Mathamagical?"

"Yeth, Mathamagical."

Ben looked perplexed, "I've never heard of such a place."

"I'm not surprised," retorted the snake, "until I came here I'd never heard of Earth."

Ben didn't like the idea that someone hadn't heard of Earth, especially a snake that claims to be a General. He wanted to know more.

"So what is Mathamagical anyway?" He asked with a hint of disbelief.

"It's where all the numbers and math symbols live." Adder raised himself up slightly with pride, "We live according to all the rules of maths. Other fractions live there too but in the majority it's us, the Maths Symbols, the Geometries and the Numerics."

"But you're not any of those," commented Ben, "you're a snake."

"I'm Adder, a maths symbol, look."

Adder lifted himself up until he was absolutely straight and standing on the tip of his tail. Then he started to concertina himself. The part of his body from the top of his head to the first bend was straight up, then, his body went off to the right about the same distance. After this, his body returned across to the left, back beyond the centre line before cutting back to the middle again. From the last bend to the floor was the same distance as from his head to the first bend. Adder continued to crunch himself until his body looked like a Plus sign found in adding up sums.

"There you go," he said, "Do I look like a Maths Symbol now?"

"Amazing!" Ben was stunned by the transformation, "So you really are from the land of maths."

Adder straightened himself back out. His face took on a serious expression.

"I have to return home," he looked Ben straight in the eyes, "and I want you to come with me?"

Ben looked surprised.

"Me," he said pointing a finger into his chest, "but what could I do there, I'm rubbish at maths?"

"I wasn't sent here to find someone who's good at maths." He exclaimed, "I was sent to find someone who is good at English."

Ben was bemused. First he was told that the land Adder came from was all about maths then he's told that they want someone who's good at English? It didn't make any sense to him.

Adder could see the confusion on Ben's face.

"The land of Mathamagical is a peaceful place," he began, "but trouble has been brewing. Across the Particle Valley lays the land of the Alphas. They are the letters that make up the words. For many years a feud has existed between the Alphas and the Numerics. The Alphas claim that they have evidence showing that the Numerics want to wipe all letters off the map. This is of course, untrue."

"And what has this got to do with you coming here?"

"I'm getting to that," continued Adder, "three days before I came here, the Alphas sent a message; an ultimatum. They said the Numerics had until the 20th night of the 10th month to surrender their lands or they will attack. Do you know what would happen if they do this?"

Ben thought for a second then answered "No."

"There will be no more numbers."

The look coming back from Ben told Adder that he didn't understand the implications of this scenario.

"If there were no more numbers everything would be words. Instead of 5," Adder drew the number 5 in the air with his tail, "You'd have FIVE," again the snake used his tail, this time he spelt out the word, "think how long it would take you to write down your phone number?"

"So if the Alphas get into your city," questioned Ben, "numbers just wouldn't exist?"

"All numbers will be replaced with letters, it will be the unthinkable."

Ben pondered all this for a moment, a talking snake telling him about Letters wiping out Numbers in a battle for land, Why not? he thought.

"So," Ben said sheepishly, "what has this got to do with me?"

Adder slithered back and forth like a person pacing up and down when they're talking to a group of people. It reminded Ben of his History teacher Miss Kurtis.

"The council of the Prime Numbers found something in the old formulas that referred to a place called Alpha Beta." Adder explained "They think this could help defeat the Alphas and defend the city."

Ben wasn't sure what to think about this, or what formulas were, so he just nodded his head in a polite way to tell Adder to carry on with his story.

"A party of numbers and symbols were sent to investigate the site described in the scrolls."

"What did they find?" asked Ben.

"A door."

"A door?"

"Yeth a big door with an alphabet keyboard next to it," Adder drew in a deep breath, "and that's not all."

Now Ben was intrigued. "What else was there?"

Adder leaned towards Ben and whispered "A rhyme."

"And you think," Ben said pointing at the snake, "that the rhyme is a code to unlock the door?"

Adder smiled.

"So you just need to break the code," Ben paused for a moment as he questioned his choice of words, "and everything's okay?"

"According to formulas, whatever is behind that door will bring harmony between the Alphas and the Numerics."

Ben didn't want to sound stupid by asking the next question he had in his head however, he knew if he didn't ask it he'd never understand what Adder was trying to get at.

"Why don't you crack the code and open the door?"

"Because, my dear boy," Adder tilted his head down to look at the floor, "in the land of maths there's no one who can solve an English problem."

"What about the Alphas?" Asked Ben

"We've tried telling them that their evidence must be wrong and that we've found something but they won't listen," Adder looked Ben straight in the eyes, "they think it's some sort of trap. Whatever they've read, it has convinced them that the Numerics want a war. This rhyme is our last chance of stopping that."

Ben found the idea intriguing; he liked word puzzles and if he could help stop a war by completing one, even better!

"Can you remember the rhyme?" he asked trying to hide his enthusiasm.

"I have committed it to memory; I thought whomever I found would ask." Using his tail to shield his mouth Adder gave a little cough to clear his throat.

∞

"My first is in MURDER but not in CROW,
My second's in LEAVE but not in GO.
My third is in LIGHT and the first of TEN.
My fourth's not in EGG but is in HEN.
I finish in START but never in TIME,
I'm a lesson to all here endeth the rhyme."

"I know how this works," said Ben full of confidence.

"Really?" Adder was getting excited.

"Yes. Each letter of the code is in each line of the rhyme with the last line being a sort of clue." Ben started to explain, "My first is in MURDER but not in CROW, means, the first letter of the code is in the word MURDER but not in the word CROW." Ben thought about it for a moment, "So it must be M, U, D or E. R is in both words so it can't be that"

The biggest smile any snake could muster appeared on Adders face, his eyes lit up and widened.

"I'll make you a deal," Adder said, "You come and help Mathamagical and I'll teach you everything you need to know about maths as we travel through the lands and the city."

He extended his tail towards Ben as if it was a hand being offered in friendship. Ben pondered the idea. It would be an adventure. He took the end of Adder's tail in his right hand and shook it in the way people would shake hands.

"Deal!" Ben was now smiling, "but how are we going to get there?"

Adder slithered over to the back of the classroom. Ben followed his movements with the torch. In the middle of the skirting board, at the back of the room, Ben could see a small door. It was about the height of the skirting board and the width of a normal electrical plug socket.

Ben had never seen the door there before and was curious about how it had got there. Adder explained that it had always been there it was just nobody had ever noticed it.

"So how come I can see it now when I wasn't even looking for it?" Ben quizzed his new friend.

"Simple," replied Adder, "you noticed it because I was looking at it. Now come over here so I can measure you."

Ben walked over to the door in the skirting board. Even though he was now closer to it somehow it looked smaller. Adder had found a tape measure from somewhere and was busily measuring the height of the door.

"Fifteen centimetres," he turned to look at Ben, "how tall are you?"

Ben shrugged his shoulders, "I don't know, about five feet?"

"Not in feet, in centimetres?"

"I don't know." Ben was getting agitated by the question.

"What do you want to know for? And where does that door go?"

"The door," replied Adder, getting Ben to hold one end of the tape, "leads to Mathamagical. Now just hold that to the top of your head." Adder stooped down holding the other end of the tape to Ben's foot, "one hundred and fifty centimetres thank you. The reason I need your height is so I can scale you down to fit through it."

Ben didn't like the sound of this. The door was very small and from what Adder had said Ben deduced he was going to be shrunk, and by the looks of it he was going to be shrunk down very small. Ben voiced his concerns.

"It's only small from your point of view," said Adder. "When I came here everything was big. I had to scale myself up."

"But how do you shrink things?"

"You use a Mathamagical spell." Adder was suddenly holding a book with an old, deep red cover decorated with gold banding on its thick, rounded spine. With his tail, Adder opened the book.

"This one's called the Scale to Ratio."

"The what to what?" Ben was beginning to wish he hadn't asked.

"Scale to Ratio. Okay you're one hundred and fifty centimetres tall and the door is fifteen centimetres tall."

"OK."

"If you divide one hundred and fifty by fifteen you get ten. That means you are ten times bigger than the door." Adder looked at Ben waiting for a response but all he got back was a blank expression. "Right, look at it this way. If you were to lie on the floor and I was to place blocks the same size as the door end to end next to you, it would take ten blocks to equal your height."

Suddenly Ben smiled and Adder knew he understood.

"So if I'm to fit through the door," Ben was sure he had this right.

"Yeth."

"You have to make me," Ben paused to count to ten before hitting Adder with his answer, "ten times smaller?"

Adder smiled broadly, "By Jove! I think you've got it."

Ben felt a warm swelling of pride flow over him. He'd never got a maths question like that right before. Basic adding up and taking away he'd got right but never one about scale.

Adder told Ben to sit down in front of the door. Ben did as he was asked and sat cross legged. Adder began to read from the book.

"Ten centimetres on Ben is equal to one centimetre on the door,"

"Isn't a spell supposed to rhyme?" interrupted Ben.

"Not Mathamagical spells." Adder gave Ben a hard stare then continued, "ten to one, one to ten"

Ben started to laugh, "Now's the time to scale down Ben."

"Stop that!"

"Sorry," Ben was doing his best to restrain his giggles, "I just thought it should rhyme."

"Well it shouldn't," The snake cleared his throat, "ten to one, one to ten, Scale down Ben Small to this ratio."

With the last word uttered Ben could feel a strange twisting feeling in his stomach. First it felt like a tickle, then he felt sick, this was followed by warmth spreading from his tummy and out across his entire body. The light on the torch began to grow and everything around him seemed to move up and away from him.

Before he knew what was happening the feelings stopped. He took a moment to gather his bearings. The door was still there in the skirting board only now it was the right size. He could see the details on it better now. The number one was carved into its thick, heavy, light blue painted wood. The door looked to be completely flush with the skirting and Ben could understand how it would have gone unnoticed before. Unless you knew that it was there, it would just look like an off coloured part of the board. Though why he had to be so close to it before he realised how uninteresting it was to look at heaven only knows.

He turned to look at the classroom. Everything was so big, he'd never have imagined that only ten times bigger would be so huge. He didn't notice Adder shrinking, he just realised the snake was there next to him; only now, Adder was the same size as he was. Ben felt better about this, travelling with a snake by his ankles would have felt weird but now he was at eye level it somehow made it Okay.

"Are you ready?" asked Adder with his tail on the handle of the door.

Ben nodded and, with a click, Adder opened the door. Ben had to shield his eyes; the light was as bright as the hottest day of summer. Adder entered Mathamagical. Ben took a deep breath and counted to ten. He quoted his Gran "In for a penny, in for a pound" and through the door he walked.

1x3=3

2x3=6

3x3=9

4x3=12

5x3=15

6x3=18

7x3=21

8x3=24

9x3=27

10x3=30

Chapter

3

three

∞

Chapter Three

Ben stepped into the light, stretching out before him,, for as far as his eyes could see was the land of Mathamagical; at his feet lay a bright green path made of green bricks. Each brick was laid perfectly, and at a very exact angle to the others.

He scanned the landscape. Everything on the right-hand side of the path was black. The bushes, which were shaped like various mathematical symbols, were black; the grass was slightly lighter and covered with numbers, but most definitely black and the birds, gathering black math symbol shaped leaves and black twigs to make a black nest high in a black multiply sign tree, were black. Even the rolling hills dipping and rising like the humps of a roller coaster disappearing off into the distance were black.

Ben turned his attention to the left-hand side of the path. It was like looking at a mirror image. Everything was in exactly the same place. The tree the birds were nesting in, was exactly the same distance from the path as it was on the right, except it was red. Everything was red. The only other difference was the numbers on the red grass. They were the exact same numbers in the very same positions as on the right only they had a small minus sign in front of them.

Adder had moved further up the path and was stood, well as much as a snake can stand, next to a wooden signpost. Ben walked up to see what the sign said. As he did he turned back to look at the hole they had just stepped out of. A moment of confusion followed, not only had the hole completely disappeared leaving even more hills with the green path cutting through them and running off to the horizon, but everything on the right of path was black and everything on the left was red. 'That's not right!' he thought.

He turned back towards Adder. Again, everything on the right of the path was black and everything on the left was red. Adder used the tip of his tail to beckon Ben over to him. The boy ran up the path. Adder could see by the bemused look Ben was carrying that he wasn't happy about something. "What's up?" hissed Adder.

"I can't tell which way I'm facing," replied Ben with a worried croak to his voice, "I look that way and everything on the right is black and everything on the left is red, then I spin around and it's still the same"

Ben gave Adder a stern look.

"It shouldn't be like that, it should be the opposite. When I look back the black should be on my left and the red on my right."

"Dear boy," Adder said shaking his head, "you're in Mathamagical now." He pointed at the path with his tail, "This is the Zero path that leads to the city of Mathamagical."

"And?"

"That over there," he said pointing to the right, "is the positive lands, and that," now pointing to the left at the red country side, "is the negative lands."

"I still don't get it?"

Adder smiled, "Everything to the left of Zero is negative and everything to the right of Zero is positive. It doesn't matter which way you're looking at it, it's always the rule."

"Oh," exclaimed Ben with a realisation, "so because positive numbers are always on the right of zero the black lands are always on the right of the Zero path."

"That's it."

Ben looked thoughtful, "So how do you know which way you're going?"

"You look at the signs."

Adder pointed to the wooden signpost. A round pole about half the size of Ben was sticking out of the ground with another piece of wood cut in the shape of an arrow nailed two thirds of the way up. The arrow pointed down the hill and had the word 'MATHAMAGICAL' painted on it in big yellow letters.

"Why is it spelt with an A?" Quizzed Ben.

This time Adder was the one looking confused, "What do you mean?"

"Well," continued Ben, "mathematics is spelt M A T H E M A T I C S, so I would have thought Mathamagical would follow the same rule?"

"Oh," smiled Adder, "It does when you're talking about casting spells but this is the name of the city and the lands so it's spelt different."

Ben was satisfied with this answer as, in his experience, place names can be spelt anyway anyone wants to when they are named in the first place so why should this be any different.

"Come on!" Adder said moving off down the path in the direction the arrow was pointing, "This way."

Ben stood for a moment wondering if this was all real or just some kind of strange dream.

"Whatever it is," he said to himself, "I'd better follow or I'll get lost."

So off he hurried to catch up with his snake friend and the two of them headed towards the city of numbers, the city of Mathamagical.

They had been walking for what felt to Ben like about half an hour when Adder suddenly stopped.

"Look," he said pointing ahead of them, "The City."

Ben squinted to try and see further. There on the edge of his sight he could just make out a tower. "You must have better eyes than me," he said to Adder, "I can just about see some sort of tower."

"Sorry, it's just…" Adder looked down at the path, with a sombre tone to his voice, "I've been away so long that I got excited at the mere sight of any part of my home"

Ben understood and felt bad for being unenthusiastic.

"No Adder, I'm sorry. It looks lovely"

"Oh it is," Adder sounded more excited again, "It's wonderful. You're going to love it, I'm sure."

Ben smiled "I'm sure I will as well"

The two stood in silence of a moment and admired the view. A flock of black birds flew off towards the city over the on the right, at the same time an exact same number of red birds flew in exactly the same way in exactly the same direction on the left. Ben had got used to the positive and negative sides of the path by now and just enjoyed the sight with no confusion.

Everything seemed so peaceful that Ben forgot for a moment the reason he was there. It was hard to believe that the city he could just about see was under threat. Adder started to advance down the path again.

Ben had seen many buildings in the distance during walks with his stepfather. By the look of how far away the tower was he reckoned it would take them about an hour to get there. He took a deep breath and, shaking off any doubts he had about the reality of his situation, strode forward to join his new friend.

The two of them walked, and slithered along the twisting turning green path making good pace. Adder told stories about growing up in the city, and Ben listened, taking in every detail with an eager ear. He was so fascinated by Adder's tales, full of youthful enthusiasm. that he didn't notice how long they'd been walking, nor did he see the city gates growing as they got closer. It wasn't until Adder told him to look that the entrance to the city took his undivided attention.

The city gates were now fully visible, two monstrous metal blocks, gold in colour and standing over thirty metres tall. Carved in to the middle of each of them was the motto of the city. It looked like a figure eight lying on its side. Ben was in awe! Stretching out from either side of the gates was the great wall of the city. Equal in height to the gates, the solid grey stone battlements cut across the positive and negative lands forming a formidable barrier.

Ben pointed at the carving on the gates.

"What's that mean?" he asked.

"That's our motto," replied Adder, "Infinite, without end, forever."

"How can anything be without an end?"

"Numbers dear boy, numbers are infinite."

Ben looked perplexed, "How?"

Adder racked his brain to try and explain it. "What's the biggest number you can think of?" he asked Ben.

"Ummmm", Ben thought hard, "Nine hundred thousand trillion, trillion million billion." He looked at Adder with a smug smile. "There can't be a bigger number than that."

"Add one." retorted Adder.

∞

"What?"

"Nine hundred thousand trillion, trillion million billion, plus one. That's a bigger number."

Ben looked thoughtful, trying to figure out if he'd just been beaten in a test, "Yes but then..."

Adder interrupted, "Then add another, and then another, and then..."

"But you could keep saying that forever?"

Adder smiled to indicate that Ben had now understood, "Infinite."

Ben did in fact now understand. There was no end to numbers, there couldn't be.

"And..." continued Adder, "that is the motto of Mathamagical. The city of numbers is without end, it is forever, or so we thought."

The advancing armies of the Alphas, Ben remembered. Adder wriggled up to the gates and, with the end of his tail, banged on them. The knocking made a thunderous booming sound that echoed in every direction. You'd never had thought that a snake, Adder's size, could make such a racket. The right-hand gate opened inwards. A funny little creature, half the size of Ben and looking like an upside-down horseshoe with feet that stuck out sideways, hopped out. Adder bent down and said something that Ben couldn't quite hear. He thought Adder said, "I have found him" but couldn't be sure.

Adder looked over to Ben and called him towards the entrance. Sheepishly, Ben moved towards the opening. Upon getting there, the upside-down horseshoe spoke. He had a rigid, authoritarian voice that commanded respect. Each word was pronounced hard and fast with short but definite gaps between them.

"Good to meet you, Mr Small, sir."

Ben returned the compliment with a more humble tone, "Nice to be here."

Adder referred to the horseshoe as guardsman and asked him for safe passage for himself and his companion into the city. The guard deliberately stepped to one side stamping his foot down like a soldier standing to attention as he arrived at his new position. Adder gestured for Ben to enter first.

Hesitantly, Ben advanced through the gap in the gates.

Adder nodded at the guard then followed. The guard turned in a military fashion, returned through the gates and slammed them shut with a loud and very deep echoing boom.

Beyond the gates, Ben found himself in a large room. It reminded him of an old castle with its high walls and cold stone. Running around the room were more of the horseshoe guards. They all seemed to have somewhere to be and were very determined to be there. Adder came up next to Ben.

"This is the guard house." he said like a tour guide.

"And these are the guards?" replied Ben gesturing to the scurrying horseshoe shaped men.

"These are the Ohms." His words were full of pride, "they are our resistance against attack."

"But they don't have any weapons?" exclaimed Ben.

"They don't need any. The more Ohms there are the less gets through."

"Defending by numbers."

"Defending by numbers?" questioned Adder, "This is defending by Ohms."

"No I meant by amount. We learnt about it in history."

Ben was good at history, English and history they were is two best subjects. He was fascinated by how long ago everything was. His favourite period was the Middle-Ages; knights on horseback, kings and queens, enormous armies in mammoth battles over castles and land. The Ohms sort of reminded him of those times.

He explained all this to Adder; how soldiers dressed in armour, carrying huge swords and axes, would run across fields at each other. Ben really liked those bits. Adder was genuinely enthralled by these stories. He particularly liked the way Ben would move about and throw his hands in the air to explain how large a weapon was or how sweeping the battlefield would be.

"Compared to the way we do battles," piped up a stern commanding voice from behind Ben, "it sounds positively barbaric!"

Ben turned round to see one of the Ohms, only instead of being all one colour this one had three white diamond shapes down each side. Ben didn't care for the way this Ohm had interrupted him in such an abrupt manner.

"And who might you be?" he snapped not liking the word barbaric.

"I am Captain Fraction," even though he didn't have any eyes that Ben could see, Ben knew the Captain was looking at him in a very stern way, "And you will call me SIR!"

The assertiveness used in the word sir made Ben jump.

"Sorry sir, I mean Captain, um, sir." He wasn't sure how to address him now.

"Stop being such a square root Captain." The familiar tone of Adder's voice made Ben feel a bit calmer, "Leave the boy alone, he's here to help us."

"General Adder," the Captain suddenly went rigid. Ben figured he must have been standing to attention. "I didn't know you were back?"

"Back and successful," Adder had more of an air of authority about him, "and you will refer to our guest as Mr Small and me as sir."

"Sorry sir, Mr Small." Ben liked the fact that the Captain now sounded more humble, "It's just with those dirty Alphas and..."

"I understand Captain." Adder interrupted with sympathy in his voice, "Tell me, is the great race still on today?"

"Yes sir."

"You've got to see the great race," Adder said to Ben, "We have it every year. I thought it was today but I couldn't be sure."

"But the Alphas and the door?" questioned Ben.

"Plenty of time, the armies aren't due to arrive until this evening."

Ben was surprised by the lack of urgency but figured Adder was just trying to make the Captain feel more relaxed.

"Well Captain, I'm sure there are plenty of things you need to be getting on with?"

"Yes sir, and welcome back sir."

Adder smiled.

"And Mr Small, I wish you all the best, good luck."

Ben smiled as well but wasn't sure if he should have done.

Captain Fraction went about his business ordering the other Ohms to do this and that. Adder pointed to a small door on the other side of the room. "This way," He motioned to Ben and slithered off towards it.

Ben thought about the first line of the riddle: "M, U, D or E?"

"Come on!" shouted Adder.

Ben turned his head to look over towards the door where Adder was standing, waved his hand and ran over to him.

Adder opened the door, "It's time to see the city."

1x4=4

2x4=8

3x4=12

4x4=16

5x4=20

6x4=24

7x4=28

8x4=32

9x4=36

10x4=40

Chapter
4
four

∞

Chapter Four

The two emerged from the fort entrance onto the street. Wide-eyed, Ben took a moment to absorb his new surroundings. Beautiful ornate buildings, almost the same height as the outer wall, stood side by side. Only the roads, leading deeper into the city, broke their smoothness. Everything was perfect; the slight curve of the road that ran inside the wall was replicated in the buildings. In each direction both left and right, Ben could see the road, buildings and outer wall bend off into the distance with precise geometric measurement.

The colours were bright and cheerful. The building painted in reds and blues, the pavement a lovely yellow and the road a slightly brighter green than the Zero path. Everywhere he looked he could see Numbers and Maths Symbols busying themselves, all with somewhere to go and something to do. The vehicles all looked like larger Maths Symbols.

A giant divide sign pulled up to a halt outside the building opposite, hissing like a bus stopping to drop off and pick up passengers. A door opened in the side of the lower dot and a multitude of different coloured numbers disembarked.

This was the outskirts of the city and it was alive with activity. The noise of the street wasn't dissimilar to that of a city or town centre back home. The vehicles all made engine noises and the low but defiant drone of many conversations filled the air. Ben took in a deep breath through his nose, no smells; the air was very clean and crisp.

Adder tapped Ben on the shoulder.

"Come on, we've got some people to see."

"Oh," Ben sounded surprised, "you call them people too."

Adder scrunched his eyebrows together, "Of course."

Ben wasn't sure why he thought they'd be called something different he just did. Adder turned and started to move off down the road. Ben took another quick look round then followed.

"This is the south circular," Adder explained, "We need to get into the centre.

It's rush hour so it'll be quicker to walk."

Ben wasn't clear what time of day it was here. He thought it must have been after midnight when they left the school, but this place bore no resemblance to the one they left, so it could be anytime. He didn't mind walking, it gave him a better chance to see more of the city, and it gave him time to think about the rhyme code.

They crossed the road and turned right down one of the main streets. More large brightly coloured buildings overlooked the passing traffic and pedestrians. Ben started to notice that, as they walked down the street, the Numbers and Symbols were turning to look at him. This made him feel uneasy and he started to get self-conscious about what he looked like. Was his hair a mess? Did his clothes look shabby? Was there a bogey hanging from his nose? Ben pulled the handkerchief out of his pocket and wiped it under his nostrils just in case.

"Adder," he said very timidly, "Why is everyone staring at me?"

Adder smiled, "Don't worry, they've just never seen a boy before, or a girl for that matter"

The realisation hit Ben, of course, just as they all looked weird and different to him, he must also look as odd and out of place to them. He felt a bit better about it though, he still didn't like attracting the attention.

They'd been walking for about quarter of an hour when Adder stopped. He was looking at a green door at the top of about ten concrete steps that led into a bright purple building.

"Here we are," exclaimed Adder, "3.141593 Tangent Avenue"

"Who lives here?"

"My good friend, Pi."

"Pie, what as in apple pie?" questioned Ben.

"No," replied Adder, "P, I, no E on the end."

"Oh," Ben was none the wiser. Sounds like pie only spelt different.

Adder climbed the steps and, with his tail, pressed the big brass button at the side of the door. From deep within the building the faint tinkling sound of the doorbell could just be heard. Ben joined Adder at the top of the steps. They stood in silence for a moment then Adder rang the bell again.

""Maybe he's out?" said Ben leaning against the door.

Just as his shoulder rested against the green paint work, the door flew open. Ben had shifted most of his weight onto the side against the door so, when the door wasn't there anymore, his weight continued to fall into the space. Ben disappeared through the doorway and landed on the hallway carpet with a bump. Embarrassed, he looked up.

Standing over him was a curious shape, two inward curving legs and a slight S shaped line across the top that stuck out at both ends. The figure bent down to talk to him in a deep knowledgeable tone.

"Are you okay?" it said.

"Yes, thank you." Ben replied picking himself up.

"You took a bit of a knock there."

"Honestly, I'm fine." Ben lied. His shoulder was hurting from the fall but he didn't want to be any bother. He rubbed the pain and stood up.

"Hello Pi." Adder smiled at the strange shape.

"Adder! You're back." Pi's tone had become more excited, "and with good news I hope?"

"I would like to introduce you to Ben." Adder extended his tail to gesture to Ben. "He's an English expert."

"I wouldn't say I was an expert." Ben added, feeling humble and slightly embarrassed.

"Compared to us," boomed Pi, "You're an expert. Now please, won't you join us for tea?"

"Us?" questioned Adder, "Who else is here?"

Pi smiled, "We're having the annual pre-race meeting of the Round Circle committee."

The Round Circle is the committee that comes up with the ideas for all the major events in Mathamagical. They started up years ago to run the first Great Race. Everyone was so pleased with their efforts that they started to meet up once a month to discuss other similar events. The Great Race now had its own committee. The members of the Round Circle were guests of honour every year, even though they don't have anything to do with the running of it anymore. And every year they had a pre-race meeting, not to discuss anything just to get together and have some tea before the festivities.

Pi led Ben and Adder into the committee room. In the middle of the room sat a large, perfectly round table. Around the table sat three other shapes, one circle, one line the same height as the circle and another line half the size of the first line.

"Let me introduce you." Pi started to walk around the table in a clockwise direction. "This is Sir Cumferance," he said stopping behind the circle.

"Nice to meet you." Greeted the circle.

Pi continued round, stopping behind the taller of the two lines, "This is Dye Ameter,"

The tall line had what sounded to Ben like a Welsh accent, "'ello."

"And this," Pi moved round yet again this time stopping at the short line, "is Ray Dius"

The short line waved at the guests.

"Where's Mr P Rimeter?" Asked Adder.

"Oh," answered Dye, "he's gone for a walk around the outside of the stadium."

Pi sat down in the chair next to Ray Dius.

"Everyone here knows Adder and what he's been doing," Pi gestured to Ben, "This is Ben. The expert Adder has found to help with the Alpha Beta."

The other three members of the committee clapped their hands together in appreciation of Adder's find. Ben was beginning to find the attention uncomfortable again.

Ben and Adder sat next to each other. In the centre of the table there was a small tea set. Sir Cumferance, Dye Ameter, Ray Dius and Pi already had a cup each. Adder reached into the middle and with a sweep of his tail slid two cups, the tea pot, milk jug and sugar bowl over to their end.

The teacups were like normal teacups, white with a royal blue infinity symbol on the side. Using his tail Adder picked up the blue spherical shaped teapot decorated with a white infinite symbol and filled each of the cups three quarters of the way up. After returning the teapot to the table he picked up the milk jug, this was the same shape and colour as the teapot only it was smaller and didn't have a lid.

"Milk?" he asked Ben.

"Yes please."

Adder tilted the jug and poured in the milk. Ben watched as the white liquid swirled in the brown of the tea.

"Thank you." He said to tell Adder that was enough.

Ben picked up the tongs sticking out of the sugar bowl and added two lumps to his drink. He stirred the mixture with a small silver spoon then looked up at the others around the table. They were all staring back at him. He turned to Adder who was just putting the finishing touches to his own beverage.

"So," started Ray Dius, "you're an English expert then?"

Ben felt shy, "I wouldn't call myself..."

"Yeth he is," interrupted Adder.

Ben didn't care for the intrusion of his response and looked at Adder with disappointment. Adder turned to look at Ben. He had a proud smile on his face which very quickly disappeared as soon as he saw the look Ben was giving him.

"Though," the snake continued, "he wouldn't call himself that."

Dye stood up, clasped his hands behind his back, and started to stroll around the table. The line's posture reminded Ben of his headmaster and when this taller of the two lines began to speak, Ben dipped his head in order not to make any kind of eye contact.

"The thing is Ben," started Dye, "it is Ben?"

Ben nodded and muttered "yes sir."

"Good," Dye had stopped behind Sir Cumferance, "the thing is Ben, you may not consider yourself to be an expert in English, but the General here," he gestured toward Adder then continued his walk, "believes you've got a better chance of opening this door and getting the Alpha Beta than anyone here."

He was half way round the table by the time he finished this statement. Pi, Ray Dius and Adder all nodded in agreement. Dye continued his stroll and his speech.

"I have seen the door described in the old formulas and I have read the puzzle." He paused just as he completed a full circuit and looked at Ben, "I have tried every mathematical solution I know and to be honest is just doesn't make sense."

The line started walking again.

"Well the thing is," replied Ben, "the puzzle is all about finding the right letter and has nothing at all to do with numbers."

"You see," said Ray with a confirming tone, "An expert!"

Ben pulled a frown at this; he really didn't like being made a fuss of even if it was for being good at something this time. He watched Dye Ameter stroll round the table; it reminded Ben again of the headmaster at his school. He would often walk up and down his office with his hands behind is back whenever he was trying to make a point. It usually involved a story showing some kind of example of how not to behave.

"If you continue down this path you have chosen you'll end like my old school chum Randy," he would start, "he behaved as you have just done, never listened to what anyone told him and now he's in prison."

Ben shuddered at the thought and started to pay attention to what was happening in the room again. Dye was on his third revolution of the group.

"...So what we need to do is take master Ben here to see the Prime Numbers, he can meet them at the great race."

Dye had just completed his latest lap and was just starting his fourth when Pi suddenly stood up.

"Now now Dye," he said with the tone of a parent telling their child to calm down, "It's time to sit down."

"Really?" Said Dye, "But I'm sure I've only been round twice?"

"No, three and a bit."

"Who am I to argue with Pi?" Dye muttered to himself as he returned to his seat.

Pi's instruction to the taller line had Ben puzzled. 'Why would Pi stop Dye Ameter walking more than three times round the table?' the boy pondered, 'and why would Mr Ameter do what Pi told him?' These questions were far too great for Ben to keep just in his head, so he leaned towards Adder and vocalised them so that the others at the table couldn't hear him.

Adder, realising that his human friend wished for discretion, whispered the answers.

"The table is a circle," he hissed quietly, "Dye Ameter is always the same height as the width of a circle and Pi," he said gently pointing under the table across at Pi, "determines the amount of times Dye Ameter can go round the outside of a circle."

"But what if the circle is bigger or even smaller? Can he go round it more or less depending on the size?" Ben questioned.

Adder smiled, as he does when he knows Ben is beginning to understand something, "no, it's always the same amount of times."

A strange curiosity washed over Ben, he felt that he needed to know about this, only this time he would be brave about it. He looked across the table at Pi and with a very determined tone asked:

"So how many times can Dye Ameter go round a circle?"

If you've ever had the feeling that you wish you hadn't done something however innocent your action or harmless your question may have been you will have some idea of how Ben suddenly felt. All conversation round the table stopped, Dye, Ray, Sir Cumferance and Pi all turned with perfect synchronicity towards the inquisitor. Ben felt the best course of action here would be to continue and see if he was right with the thought in his head.

"Is it three?"

A big smile spread out across Pi's face and just as he was about to speak, Dye interrupted.

"It's written on his door," he said in a slightly disgruntled yet ironic way "and he never lets me forget it."

Ben scrunched up his nose as he tried to recall the number of the house.

"You mean, 3.141, erm 5..."

"Yes 3.141593," interrupted Sir Cumferance saving Ben from straining his brain any more, "well remembered."

"Well," said Pi, "It has a few more decimal places but that's all that would fit on the door without looking stupid."

"How many decimal whatsits?" asked Ben, feeling less uncomfortable now. He knew that decimal places where the numbers after the full stop in a number, only his brain wouldn't allow him to say the words properly for some reason.

"A great number," said Pi, "a great number indeed."

Pi rose from the table and started to walk towards the door.

"Come," he said, "or we'll all be late for the race."

The sound of scraping chairs filled the air as everyone around the table, including Ben and Adder stood up and followed Pi.

The party left 3.141593 Tangent Ave and turned right. The streets were empty, not a number or symbol could be seen anywhere, everyone had gone to the stadium. Ben could tell that they where heading in a direction away from the city wall and surmised that they were heading towards the centre.

After about ten minutes of brisk walking a sight that Ben could never have begun to imagine came in to view. The stadium, taller than any sports arena he had ever seen before, for real or on the television, rose from the ground to a height that would dwarf Big Ben, its sides curving away to meet each other round the other end and form a perfect circle. Numbers and symbols queued by the buildings many entrances and, from the echoing noise coming from within, Ben could tell it was already pretty full.

The members of the Round Circle led Ben and Adder to a very well decorated door which bore the sign 'Athletes, VIP's and Dignitaries only'. The two Ohms, who were standing either side of the entrance, came to attention

∞

as Pi advanced towards them. The one to the right opened the door allowing the party access to the arena.

Inside they walked down a long, tall and very wide corridor. At the far end Ben could see daylight and from this opening he could also hear the sound of a large number of people, the people of Mathamagical.

"Is that where the race is taking place?" he asked Adder pointing towards the light and the noise.

"Yeth," replied Adder, "come on let us go and get our seats."

1x5=5

2x5=10

3x5=15

4x5=20

5x5=25

6x5=30

7x5=35

8x5=40

9x5=45

10x5=50

Chapter
5
five

∞

Chapter Five

All available space in the stadium was filled with numbers and symbols. Every which way Ben looked all he could see were the bright colours of the citizens of Mathamagical jostling for a better view of the track. The noise of the crowd was incredible; creating an atmosphere Ben felt he could almost touch.

The track everyone was so desperate to see lay in the middle of the round green which the stands surrounded. It ran from one side to the other, white with black lines measuring one metre sections of the hundred metre course. It reminded Ben of the rulers they used to measure things with at school, only much bigger.

The maths folk were so full of cheer and excitement it was hard to believe this place was under threat of attack. Their singing and laughter could be not only heard but felt. Ben was stunned, his eyes wide open, his ears full of the noise and his fingers tingled, he had never experienced anything like this before.

"Adder was right," he whispered to himself, "this is truly magical."

Adder slithered up beside him. He could see the look of wonderment on Ben's face which made him smile.

"Come on," he said, pulling Ben's arm with his tail, "I have some people I want you to meet."

He led Ben out onto the track area. Now Ben was paying more attention he noticed a smaller stand positioned next to the track, halfway down its length. Seated in the enclosure were four numbers, though they weren't the same bright colours he'd already seen. From this distance he couldn't make out what numbers they were. Ben turned to look back in the direction they had come from. Sir Cumferance, Dye Ameter, Ray Dius and Pi were following them across the green.

Turning back again to look where he was going Ben could see the stand more clearly. He could also see the numbers in the small stand better, 2, 3, 5 and 7. They weren't colours as such, more metal. 2 was a bright gold, 3 a shimmering silver, 5 a deep bronze and 7 a shiny chrome.

They reached the edge of the track. Ben could now see it was divided into two lanes with a black line separating them. The surface was very smooth and looked like plastic. They strolled across the track and climbed the four steps up into the stand.

Adder used his tail to open the door, which was a bit stiff and needed a bit more force to push open than the snake anticipated. The door jarred forward and despite his forward momentum, Adder kept his balance and grace. The numbers turned to look at them as they entered. The gold 2 greeted the General with a deep formal voice.

"Adder"

"Prime Number 2" Adder replied bowing his head to the gold number before repeating the gesture to the other numbers, 'Prime Numbers'

Ben felt awkward just standing there after forcing the door back into its hole, so he copied Adder's respectful greetings, but without saying anything. Adder introduced Ben to the Prime Numbers and did his usual explanation regarding Ben's presence though rather than declaring the boy to be an 'English Expert' this time he said Ben was going to try and help as he was 'rather good at solving English problems.' The serpent looked at Ben for approval after his new introduction. Ben felt more comfortable with this description and smiled.

"And Ben," continued Adder, "these are the Prime Numbers. They are the keepers of the formulas and Ruling Council of Mathamagical."

"Nice to meet you," Ben said bowing again.

Just as Ben dipped the top half of his body in a show of respect the door to the stand burst open hitting him on the bum, knocking him off balance and sending him stumbling forward. Despite his best efforts to regain some kind of control, Ben hit the back of the seats and, arms desperately flapping, tumbled head first into the Prime Numbers.

"There you go Sir Cumferance," boomed the voice of Pi from the doorway, "all it needed was a bit of effort."

∞

Adder quickly moved round the seats to help Ben and the fallen dignitaries. Ben was desperately apologising to the Prime Numbers whilst the said council were telling him not to worry about it and wanted to know if he was okay. Pi stood in the doorway unaware he was responsible for the kerfuffle.

"What happened here?" he enquired.

Adder, Ben and the Prime Numbers all glared at him with a look of annoyance.

"Come on Pi" the unmistakable tone of Sir Cumferance said from outside, "get out of the way."

Pi, now realising he had something to do with the chaotic scene in front of him, sheepishly entered the stand.

"Don't worry about it Pi", said 7, "these things happen."

The circle and the two lines entered and, seeing the confusion, enquired about the goings on with the same words Pi had just uttered. The very same response came from the group who were now finding some sort of order. Pi looked away, a little embarrassed; he had worked out what he had done and realised that was the second time today he had caused Ben to fall by opening a door.

All the members of the Round Circle took their seats in the second row of three. The Prime Numbers, after once again making sure Ben was alright, sat down in the front row. Ben and Adder sat at the back. The view of the race track was great, Ben could see both ends.

"Adder," Ben whispered, "why are they the Prime Numbers? Was there a vote or something?"

Adder smiled.

"No," Adder started to explain, "Prime Numbers can only be divided by themselves and 1 without leaving a remainder. There are thousands of Prime Numbers. However, these are the only single Prime Numbers."

"But what about all the other 2's 3's 5's and 7's in Mathamagical?"

"They are on standby for the ruling council should anything happen to these.

Accidents, old age, that kind of thing."

Ben thought about it for a moment.

"So all numbers that can only be divided by themselves and 1, leaving a whol number, are Prime Numbers?" asked Ben confirming to himself he understood.

"That's right" replied Adder.

"And these are the only single Prime Numbers?"

"Yeth"

"What about 1?"

"1 isn't considered a Prime Number," Adder said looking out towards the track "you're right, it can only be divided by itself and 1 but as it is 1, it can only reall be divided by itself."

"So what does that make it?"

"The beginning of everything we know in Mathamagical."

A loud click, like someone switching on a microphone, echoed round the stadium from the tannoy high in the stands. The crowd, almos immediately, fell silent. A slight cough broke the hush, just before the voice o the announcer boomed from the speakers.

"Numbers and Symbols, Shapes and Angles, please be upstanding and welcome the runners!"

The crowd cheered in unison, making a noise louder than anything Ber had ever heard. Everyone stood up in the small stand. Ben had to jostle for a good position to see the little opening at the right hand end of the ground Everybody was watching this entrance.

Squinting, Ben tried to get a good view of the athletes. For a moment he thought he must be seeing things. Emerging from the shadow of the tunnel and accepting the rapturous reception from the crowd, was, what looked like to Ben, an egg with legs and a chicken.

"It's an egg and a chicken!" exclaimed Ben to Adder.

"Yeth," Adder replied without taking his eyes off the so called runners, "this is the great race."

Ben watched as the two strode down the length of the track. All he

∞

could hear were the cheers and applause from the crowd. Everyone around him in the small stand were on their feet clapping loudly.

"But why?" asked Ben, "Why an egg and a chicken?"

Adder turned to Ben with a questioning expression.

"Well how else are we going to find out which came first unless we race them?"

Ben could feel the perplexed look he was now wearing. His first thought was how preposterous it was to hold a race to see which came first the chicken or the egg. Then he thought a bit harder about it.

"The egg is laid by the chicken," he whispered to himself, "and the chicken comes from the egg."

The problem put this way made his head hurt. The idea of racing them to find out once and for all didn't seem so silly now.

The crowd fell suddenly silent. Ben look towards the track, he could see the egg and chicken at the start line, waiting for the signal to go. A rather official looking number 5 stood by the side of the track. It raised its left arm; Ben could clearly see the starting pistol in its left hand. BANG!

The chicken was the first to react, striding away from the start line. The egg sort of jumped on the spot before setting off in pursuit of its feathered opponent. After the first ten metres, the chicken was well ahead placing stride after long stride in a perfect rhythm. The egg on the other hand, was stumbling up the track and hardly seemed to know which way to run.

Ten metres, twenty metres, thirty metres, the chicken was in complete control. As the fowl leader passed the forty metre mark, the poor yolk filled shell was still way back on the twenty metre mark. Then something happened that got the crowd very excited. The egg seemed to gain some composure and started to close the gap. It had gained back a full ten metres on the chicken as the bird crossed the half way point.

From Ben's point of view, it seemed that as the egg got a sudden burst of speed, the chicken was beginning to look a bit tired. Sixty, seventy, eighty, the egg was catching fast and, as the ninety metre mark trampled underfoot, both the chicken and the egg were neck and neck.

∞

Now the egg was taking the lead. Five metres to go and, was Ben seein things, the chicken was gaining ground. Four metres, three metres, surely th was the egg's race, two metres, one metre the chicken was right on top of th egg now and, to an explosion of cheers, so it looked from where Ben was sitting the two runners crossed the finish line at the same time.

"Looks like a dead heat!" exclaimed Ben in a very excited tone to the whol stand.

Pi replied with a joyful laugh to his voice, "It is every year."

"Come," said Adder, "let's go and see the judges and find out if they can get result this year?"

The Prime Numbers were the first to leave the stand, followed by th Round Circle, then Ben and Adder. By the time they got out and onto the are surrounding the track, a group of numbers with tape measures had assemble by the finish line, and by the looks of their exaggerated arm movements, the were having an argument.

"I'm telling you," said a rather animated blue number 4, "according to the lengt of the chicken's beak at the time of reaching the line, in all probability the chicke won."

"Rubbish," piped up a red number 8, "the speed the egg was moving would hav meant that the forward momentum would have easily carried it over the finis first."

All the gathered numbers then started throwing in their theories abou who had won and how to prove it. A yellow number 6 said something abou weight ratios and then, a green number 9 harped on about aerodynamics. Th din went on for a fair few minutes until the entire judging panel of numbers wa struck by silence after Ben asked one simple question.

"Why don't you take a photograph?"

Prime Number 2 stepped up, "A photograph?"

"Yes," replied Ben, "you know, with a camera."

"We are well aware of what a photograph is dear boy." The green number 9 sai in a very prudish manner.

"Why not set a camera up on the finish line and when the runners cross it take photograph?" Ben looked round expecting an interruption. It didn't come, "that way you could see which one was over the line first."

Sir Cumferance was the first the break the silence, "that is a great idea."

All the numbers started to agree that Ben had in fact come up with the solution they had all been looking for. Years of running races and arguing about whom had won, would be over.

Prime Number 5 declared that this should be announced to everyone. He took the microphone and after a couple of clicks and a bit of a whistle through the speakers, he began his address to the crowd.

"Numbers and symbols of Mathamagical," the crowd silenced, "our new friend has come up with a plan that will determine the outcome of this, the great race, once and for all time." A sudden sound, like a thousand people just drew in a deep breath, spread across the crowd, "This new idea, which will be called a photo finish, will, all being well, be applied to next year's race and we will finally answer the question."

The crowd exploded with cheers again.

"Next year," Ben said to himself, "so I'll never find out the answer."

A large white minus sign with wheels drove into the centre of the stadium and pulled to a halt. A door towards what Ben could determine was the back of the vehicle opened. The Prime Numbers moved towards the minus sign waving at the crowd as they went.

"Come on," whispered Adder to Ben, "we have to go."

Adder started to gently pull Ben toward the Prime Number's transport. Sir Cumferance, Ray Dias and Dye Ameter all called out their goodbyes.

"Good luck Ben" shouted Dye "I hope you succeed."

Ben could see Pi having a little chat with the others from the Round Circle before following Adder and himself to the minus sign.

Ben entered the vehicle first. It was much bigger inside than he had imagined. The Prime Numbers were all sitting down one side on a very comfy looking red seat. Opposite them was a similar seat which Prime Number 2 gestured to Ben to sit down on. Adder soon entered followed by Pi.

∞

"Right!" said Prime Number 5, "off to the Chamber of Formulas."

The vehicle jerked and all the passengers sitting on the red seats in the rear fell towards the back; all except Adder. His snake body provided the perfect balance required and, being as he was sitting towards the front of the vehicle, no one else fell on top of him.

After a few moments of shuffling and saying sorry to one another, the party managed to right itself again and they were soon all in deep conversation about the Alpha Beta; all except Ben. He was trying to listen to what was being said but not giving an opinion. To be honest he still wasn't sure what was going on.

He knew that he was there to figure out this code and he knew that everyone thought that this would stop the Alpha's from attacking. He wasn't sure why this would work or what they expected to find behind this door. From the conversation taking place in the back of what he thought was rather like a limousine, no one in the land of Mathamagical had any idea what was behind it either.

"I think it's a weapon?" said Number 5, "an Alpha Beta as the formulas called it."

"No," said Number 7, "I've studied the formulas really hard and it says that the Alpha Beta will bring peace between us and the Alphas."

"Weapons can bring peace?" argued 5.

"Weapons bring war not peace," Adder said with an authority, "Isn't that right Ben?" Ben just shrugged then nodded.

"Whatever it is," said 2, "it's needed to stop this silly battle from starting in the first place."

This statement they all agreed to. What was behind the door would soon be revealed was the next unilaterally approved observation. Though Ben didn't share their belief in his ability to crack the code, he did agree with the idea behind what they were saying, and just smiled at the overwhelming compliments being thrown his way.

They seemed to be travelling for ages when suddenly the vehicle stopped. Again, the passengers were dislodged from their seats; only this time they moved faster and towards the front and, this time, Adder was unable to keep upright. As Pi slid into Ben, his weight plus, Ben's forward motion caused the two to collide with the snake. The predictable outcome of this involuntary motion was that all three ended up on the floor with the Prime Numbers.

"I think we're here!" said Adder pulling himself out from underneath the pile of bodies.

As they were all brushing themselves off and yet again apologising to each other, the limousine door opened again. The Prime Numbers were the first to leave, followed by Pi. Adder smiled at Ben.

"Don't worry," he said with a reassuring tone, "I know you can do this."

Ben just smiled as Adder made his exit. He took a deep breath, told himself that he was good at English and boldly ventured out of the abruptly starting and stopping transport.

1x6=6

2x6=12

3x6=18

4x6=24

5x6=30

6x6=36

7x6=42

8x6=48

9x6=54

10x6=60

Chapter

6

six

∞

Chapter Six

The Great Hall was a formidable sight. Smooth, white marble-ish stone formed the walls and looked so bright that they seemed to emanate light. The architecture was full of every geometric shape you could think of. Triangles lined the roof whilst perfect circles formed the shapes of the windows, of which there were far too many for anyone to consider counting. A large canopy, made from the same stone as the building, protruded over the square entrance. The pillars on the front two corners connecting it to the ground, supporting its weight, formed a giant cube in the process.

Lining the sides of the grey path, leading up to the door, ten columns, five on each side of the walkway, stood two metres tall, like a giant stone guard of honour. Mounted on the top of these pillars were five pairs of perfectly curved, three-dimensional objects with solid shapes down the left and hollow outlined versions on the right.

The four faced Tetrahedron was first, mounted so that the point of the three sided pyramid made contact with the column and what would usually be the flat underside faced up towards the sky, forming a platform for the birds to rest on. The box like Cube, with its six faces was next, again mounted on a point so that all its sides were visible to the elements, this was followed by the eight faces of the Octahedron which overlooked the path, perched upon the centre column. Twelve flat surfaces made up the Dodecahedron before the spectacular Icosahedrons' twenty sides finished off this avenue of stone.

Ben looked at the shapes as the party walked towards the building. Adder told Ben the names of each shape and Ben, in turn, told Adder how many sides they had. Adder was pleasantly surprised by the young lad's knowledge. Ben explained that they looked just like the dice he used when he and his friends participated in role playing games.

"Role playing games?" asked Adder.

"Yes," said Ben with an air of authority, "It's like writing a story but you play the characters. We use dice to work out what happens."

"Sound like fun."

Ben smiled, it was fun, he thought to himself.

The large red square doors glided open to reveal a beautiful, smooth white floor with dark green walls, reaching up to the geometrically patterned ceiling. The party walked down this great corridor with only the echoing sounds of their footsteps, from those that had feet, breaking the silence. Ben felt like he was walking into a majestic temple and thought that it would be disrespectful to ask too many questions. Instead he just walked with the others, looking around at every detail.

Cut into the walls at perfectly measured distances, doorways lead off to more corridors or stairs made from the same white stone. Some of the doors were closed with signs written on them, giving clues as to what went on behind them.

Ben figured that the door reading 'Measurements Department' would be full of people doing things with millimetres, centimetres and metres. They were probably responsible for the track the Great Race was run on, he thought.

It's worth noting that this building was the first one ever built in the lands of Mathamagical and, as far as anyone could tell, Ben was the first non-resident of the lands to ever set foot in it. Even though the main corridor is open to all citizens, because the Great Hall houses the public library, most have never been. This honour was completely lost on Ben, he had no knowledge of how unique his visit was and nobody bothered to tell him.

At the end of the corridor, 2 turned to face the rest of them, this signalled everyone to stop. Ben started feeling uncomfortable again, he figured they were about to enter a room with more new people to meet, this meant more explaining to do. The enormity of the building played a big part in these feelings, new surroundings can overwhelm you at times and, on this occasion, it certainly did to Ben.

"Ben," Started 2 in a sort of half whisper, "we are about to enter the school of Mathamagical. The children will be excited to see all of us but will be very interested in you."

∞

He paused to gauge Ben's reaction. Ben wasn't sure what 2 was really talking about so just nodded politely.

"As with everyone in Mathamagical," 2 continued, "they have never seen a human before and you know how excitable children can be."

Ben nodded, again he didn't really grasp what 2 was trying to say. He just figured it would be like the schools he knew back home.

When Ben was younger, the firemen come round to see them and talk about how dangerous it was to play with matches. All the children loved seeing the firemen with their yellow helmets, big torches and black Wellington boots. They took them outside and showed them the fire engine. Ben could remember how excited he was, sitting behind the wheel of that big red truck. Maybe his presence would be as exciting for the children here, and that's what 2 was talking about.

2 turned to the door on the right of the corridor. As he pushed it open, the sound of children playing invaded the hanging silence that had surrounded them since entering the great hallway. Ben stood still as the others headed through the door. He took a deep breath, then another, before finally advancing to follow them, and then only after Adder had beckoned him to.

The room they entered was like a giant indoor playground, there were all kinds of brightly coloured equipment designed in the shapes of mathematical symbols. A climbing frame in the shape of a multiply sign, swings hanging under the left and right arms of a giant plus and a slide sloping down off the back of a great big equals; climbing, swinging, rocking and spinning on these contraptions were little numbers over numbers, like the way you would write a fraction, a number then a straight, horizontal line then another number.

Sat on either end of a seesaw, made from a divide sign with the middle line forming the plank and the dots above and below the line forming the pivot hinge, Ben could see a 3 over 5 and an 8 over 9.

"How old are they?" Ben asked Adder with a whisper.

"Well," started Adder, "that 3 over 4 on the swing is three quarters her full age."

Ben didn't understand what Adder was trying to say and the expression on his face showed this.

Adder tried to explain it a different way, "the bottom of the two number is what number they are going to be when they grow up."

"Right" Said Ben, nodding his head.

"And the top number shows how long into growing up they are." Adder pointed at another number child, "you see that 3 over 8 by the slide. Well he's 3, 8ths into becoming a full number 8. The little chap still has 5, 8ths to go."

Ben thought he was beginning to understand.

"So how long does it take to become a grown up?"

"Depends on how well they do in their education. The better they learn, the more complete they get." Adder looked proudly across the indoor school yard, "and when they are ready, they graduate and become whole numbers."

"So," Ben started in his usual, timid, fashion which he used when he was trying to see if he understood, "The top number is how many parts of the bottom number they are?"

"Yet again you are correct."

Adder's smile was so big that Pi even noticed.

"What are you smiling at Adder?"

"Oh nothing, my dear Pi, nothing."

Adder gave Ben a knowing glance which made Ben feel good about himself.

"If you want to keep secrets Adder, that's up to you?" Said Pi, obviously put out by Adders obtuse comment.

Suddenly, one of the children noticed the visitors and screamed out at the top of their voice.

"LOOK, IT'S THE PRIME NUMBERS!"

All the children stopped their climbing, swinging, rocking and spinning and came running over to the group. Their squeals of delight turned to stunned silence as they saw Ben. He felt equally unnerved at the sight of all these little fractions running towards them.

∞

From the back of the crowd, a brown number 9 wearing glasses came pushing through.

"Let me through now children," she said with an air of kind authority, "and back up a bit, we mustn't crowd our guests."

The teacher greeted the Prime Numbers with a slight curtsey before giving similar respect to Pi, Adder and Ben. The young human felt rather embarrassed by the whole situation and tried to hide himself behind Adder.

"Is that a mewman miss!?" shouted out a 4 over 9 whilst pointing directly at Ben.

"That's very rude," the teacher replied, chastising the fraction with the tone of her voice, "and the word is human!"

She gave Ben a comforting glance.

"I'm sorry about that, you know what youngsters can be like; no manners."

"That's quite alright," said Ben, peering out from behind the General.

2 stepped forward, "This is Ben," he said, "and he is our very special guest so we expect you to treat him with the same respect as you would your teacher."

Ben could feel his cheeks warm but felt brave enough to show himself a bit more to the crowd. The young numbers gasped, they, like everyone else in Mathamagical, had never seen a human. However, being so young, they showed their surprise at the sight of someone so different with sounds of amazement.

"Hello." Ben said with a little sheepish wave.

The children giggled and their teacher told them to 'hush now.' 2 explained that they were just passing through on their way to the Vault.

"A very important matter then?" was the knowing response from the teacher.

"Indeed," replied Prime Number 7.

"And how did the great race finish?" quizzed the teacher, who was unable to attend due to her duties with the children.

"Oh it was a dead heat again." piped up Pi, "but Ben here has told us how to sort it out next year."

"Clever little soul" the 9 said, smiling at Ben.

Ben hung his head and smiled. He felt a little humble at being called clever, though the teacher's smile made him feel pleased about it at the same time. I wish she was my maths teacher he thought to himself.

"Now children," the teacher said clapping her hands, "we must let our guests get on with the important matter at hand, I'm sure Ben will come back another time to tell you stories about his world?"

Ben smiled, he loved to tell stories.

"I most certainly will."

The children gave out a cheer to show their approval of this idea. Just then, a bell sounded which excited the little ones again. The teacher started to tell them all the calm down and started herding them towards a door on the other side of the play area. The children kept looking back and shouting "bye Ben" as they left. Soon the place was quiet, leaving only Pi, Adder, Ben and the Prime Numbers with the play equipment.

Adder was the first to break the silence.

"Young inquisitive minds can be very tiring."

Everyone agreed before moving on to a door on their side of the play room. As they approached, 2 took out an infinity shaped key and used it to unlock the barrier, with a loud clunk of the mechanism. Using the handle, he swung the door open revealing a short corridor which led to a set of stairs leading down below the building.

The walls looked different, darker and a slightly stale smell emanated from the entrance. Ben turned to Adder for reassurance.

"This is the way to the Vault," Adder began, recognising the unspoken question, "the only people to use this door are the Prime Numbers and The 1."

"So why is the entrance in the school yard?"

"Because no one would think of looking for it here."

It was as reasonable an answer has Ben could have hoped for.

"So," Ben said, "are the Prime Numbers and This 1 the only people allowed to see the formulas?"

"No," replied Adder, "There are also the Scholars and their assistants." He

∞

looked at Ben and smiled, "They live down here."

Ben raised his right eyebrow; to him the only thing he could do to get a real understanding of what Adder was telling him was to see it for himself. He looked back towards the door. Pi was standing at the top of the stairs looking rather impatient, he waved his hand to signal, 'Come on!' The sharpness of his hand movement showed that he was getting annoyed. Ben and Adder walked through to the top of the stairs.

"I thought you were going to stay there all day?" protested Pi.

Adder turned and bolted the door, the scrape and click of each of the three locks echoed down the stone stairwell.

"Will you come on!" said Pi.

His impatient ramblings, designed to make the two stragglers pick up the pace, reminded Ben of the White Rabbit. All Pi had to do now was say 'we're late' and his impression of Alice's timekeeping bunny would be almost perfect.

1x7=7

2x7=14

3x7=21

4x7=28

5x7=35

6x7=42

7x7=49

8x7=56

9x7=63

10x7=70

Chapter
7
seven

∞

Chapter Seven

All of the rules, which the citizens of Mathamagical lived their lives by, are calculated from the old formulas. These scriptures have been the basis of law and order for as long as numbers have existed, or at least as long as records have been kept. They are constantly read, calculated and proved by the scholars who sit in a room situated in front of the Vault's door.

No one except the Prime Numbers and The 1 are allowed to enter the Vault, not even the scholars. If they want to read any of the formulas, to check their answers they have to call on the governing bodies to extrapolate the information required. Only the highest of Numbers knows the combination to the Vault, only they can find the reference, a term used when requesting documents.

Deep below the Great Hall, in chambers older than the building itself, these tireless custodians of everything that is numbers work without rest. Checking, double checking and rechecking figures to ensure that all calculations are correct.

It was in amongst these papers that the location of the door was found, deep within the Vault, under documents so old they had gone unnoticed for several generations, this dust covered salvation, lay uncalculated.

Now it was stored, near the front of the Vault, along with a copy of the riddle combination. And it was towards these dusty old documents that Ben headed with his friend Adder, a rather grumpy Pi and the Ruling Council of this great city.

The party started descending into the labyrinth of corridors and stairs that made up the catacombs below the great building. They would go down two sets of steps, then up one, turning left then right. Ben was quite lost and had no idea where they were. Most of the time in these lands he could tell which way they were facing, north, south, east or west, even without a compass. But down here, in the dark damp corridors under the Great Hall, he could no longer be sure. By his reckoning, they were no longer under the building.

The walkways were lit by small spheres that glowed, attached to the walls about a quarter of the way down from the ceiling. There was no visible source of power; however with everything else that Ben had seen he didn't think this was too unusual.

The walls, ceiling and floor were no longer made from the beautiful white marble previously used in the Great Hall. It was now a dark grey which looked very cold and ever so slightly damp. To Ben, it looked very old and reminded him of the dungeons he had walked round with his Gran at Lancaster Castle.

They seemed to be walking for an extraordinarily long time before the corridor opened up into a room so big Ben reckoned you could get four football pitches side by side in it; this was the Chamber of Formulas. Around the walls, filing cabinets stood side by side with no gaps between them, Ben reckoned there must be tens of thousands of drawers there, if not millions.

Various numbers were running this way and that, opening drawers to either put pieces of paper in or take them out. Sat in the middle of the room rows of wooden desks, not dissimilar to those Ben used in his school, lined up sixteen wide and sixty four deep, or so Ben counted. Sat at these desks were light grey 1's and 0's (zeros), one digit per desk. The number retrieving the papers from the filing cabinets ran round to the right hand side of these columns of numbers, handed the first 1 the paper who would read it, write something on it with a pencil before handing it on to the 0 next to them. This 0 would read the paper then, with an eraser, rub something out and hand it on to the next 1.

This pattern would continue, 1's writing something and handing it to 0's, 0's rubbing things out and handing it to 1's until the paper, having been passed along all sixteen desks would be picked up by one of the other numbers and taken round to the right hand side of the next row. This time the row started with a 0 who would read it, rub something out and pass it on to a 1, and so on and so forth.

Once the paper reached the final table of the final row, one of the other running numbers would pick up the paper and return it to the filing cabinet. This paper movement was continuous, all you could hear was the sound of drawers opening and closing, rustling paper, pencils scraping and squeaking erasers.

"What's happening here?" asked Ben.

"These are the Scholars," answered Adder, "they read the formulas and calculate them. Because they keep recalculating and coming up with new numbers they have to keep revising all the other formulas."

Suddenly on the fifth row up, nine seats across, one of the 1's stood up.

"I need a reference." he demanded, "Call the Prime Numbers!"

"Um sir," said a number 4 sheepishly as he handed the 1 at the beginning of the row a piece of paper he had just retrieved from the 0 at the end of row four, "They're already here."

The 4 pointed over to the group.

"Blimey," said the 1, "That was quick."

Prime Number 3 stepped forward raising himself up to look very important.

"We are here to see the formula of the Alpha Beta"

All the numbers stopped what they were doing, even the 1's and 0's. The Prime Numbers walked over to the huge, heavy looking door on the other side of the room. About half the height of the wall and quarter of its width, the Vault door looked impenetrable. On the door, eight round knobs lined up next to a massive lever. Ben assumed these discs must be a combination lock. As the Prime Number passed row eleven the 0 on the end stood up.

"With all due respect Sir, we have tried every number system to prove that formula," he looked down at his desk, "and there is nothing we can do."

Prime Number 2 turned to look at the 0.

"General Adder has returned with Ben, a human."

The Scholars looked over at Ben, Adder and Pi. The sight of one thousand and twenty four 1's and 0's suddenly looking at him made Ben very nervous, add to that, the one hundred and twenty eight other numbers and

∞

you have enough eyes staring to make anyone's knees go a bit weak.

"He is just a boy!" said the 0.

Pi stepped forward, "He, Ben, is an English expert."

Again Ben felt embarrassed by this but was glad that Pi had spoken up for him, he didn't care for the way the 0 had referred to him as just a boy.

PI's comment was about to be added to by Ben, when the entire room in front of him, including the Prime Numbers, stopped and bowed. Ben turned to Adder but he was also stood with his head bowed and facing the other way. Unsure of what was happening, Ben turned to see why everyone was beginning to bow.

Stood in the opening of the room was a smooth, transparent with a slightly blue tint, crystal Number 1. Ben's eyes widened, he was so amazed by the sight that he never thought about copying everyone else's etiquette and bow. The Number 1 walked over to him and gently closed Ben's mouth.

"Who dared question the Prime Numbers?" the 1's voice filled the room; it was loud but not like shouting.

The 0 that had said the derogatory remark about Ben being just a boy began to speak.

"I was just..."

"Well don't!" exclaimed the crystal digit, "Time is of the essence here. The Alphas have been spotted from the wall, which means they are no more than a day away from the edge of the city."

The most respected of numbers moved slowly towards the front row of desks.

"Prime Numbers, fetch the formula from the Vault."

The Council obeyed without delay, quickly making their way to the back of the room. They fiddled with the dials then 2, with a loud clunk, turned the handle 90o down.

With the help of 3, 5 and 7, 2 pulled the door open. It must have been a metre thick. Beyond its protection was a room twice the size of the chamber. Ben could see shelves, three metres high, stacked with folders and papers going back in aisles like a supermarket.

The 1 pointed at the opinionated 0, "You can give up your desk for Ben."

The 0 backed away from his work station without as much as whisper. The 1 ushered Ben to the desk and gestured him to sit. Ben obliged as he was too scared not to.

2 entered the Vault with 7. The chamber had a very uncomfortable silence hanging over it as they all waited for the two Prime Numbers to return. After what seemed like an age they re-entered the room from the Vault holding several old pieces of parchment.

Carefully, they carried them over to the desk that Ben was sitting at and placed them in front of him. Altogether, there were nine sheets, one of which was a map and seven were numbers and calculations. One, which was the one that Ben was most interested in, had writing on it. This one was a much newer piece of paper; it had been used to record the code that would open the door to the Alpha Beta. Ben picked it up and read:

> "My first is in MURDER but not in CROW,
> My second's in LEAVE but not in GO.
> My third is in LIGHT and the first of TEN.
> My fourth's not in EGG but is in HEN.
> I finish in START but never in TIME,
> I'm a lesson to all, here endeth the rhyme."

He had been thinking about this, on and off, since they arrived here; turning the words over in his mind trying to find those letters that would form the answer. He started talking quietly to himself.

"Murder, Crow? Leave Go? First in Ten? Well the first letter of Ten, is T.

Not in Egg but is in Hen, can't be N because that would never follow T, so it must be H, TH." Ben scratched the top of his head, "In Start but not in Time that follows TH, Maybe S, THS, then, maybe A from leave? It's not in Go. Lesson to all…"

∞

Ben suddenly sat up straight.

"I've got it!"

Adder forgot protocol and rushed over pushing past The 1 as he did so. The runner numbers winced as they waited for their leader to chastise the excited snake. Not pleased, but understanding of his General's over eagerness, The 1 chose not to say anything on this occasion.

"What is it?"

"The answer is MATHS!"

"No" said the 0 that wasn't happy about letting Ben read these important documents in the first place, "The answer is a Word."

"That's what I mean," said Ben sarcastically, "The word is MATHS! Look."

He beckoned everyone round the desk.

"My first is in Murder but not in Crow that's M, the letter is in the word Murder but not in the word Crow."

He continued to explain how he got all the other letters. Adder felt so proud he almost cried. The 1 patted Ben on the back.

"Well done!" he said before turning to Adder, "General you take Ben, Pi and Prime Number 2 to the location of the door immediately."

"But I thought," said Ben, "that once I had…"

"Don't argue," ordered The 1, "we have no time to waste."

Adder picked up the map from the desk, as he did he whispered into Ben's ear.

"Just another little adventure."

Ben rose from his seat and followed Adder, Pi and Prime number 2 as they set off down the long maze of corridors and stairs back to the Great Hall again.

1x8=8

2x8=16

3x8=24

4x8=32

5x8=40

6x8=48

7x8=56

8x8=64

9x8=72

10x8=80

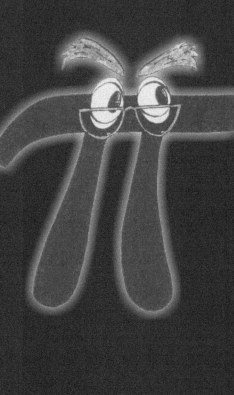

Chapter
8
eight

Chapter Eight

"So how are we going to get there?"

Ben's question to Adder was with genuine concern. On the walk back from the Vault, he was told how they had to travel to the furthest point south of the Mathamagical lands. The door they were heading towards was deep within a series of caves found at the foot of the Hypotenuse Mountains, a vast range of triangular shaped mountains so rugged that no one has ever been able to cross it and find out what's on the other side.

From what the others had been saying, Ben figured it would take over a week to get there on foot and the description of the cosine forest, that occupied the void between the city and their destination, sounded so rough that they would not be able to drive.

"You'll see." Was the only answer Adder would give, even when Ben asked for the third time with his most insistent voice.

The four of them passed back though the indoor school yard into the Great Hallway. This time, 2 led them through a door on the opposite side which opened onto a set of stairs taking them up. Ben stood at the bottom and looked up the middle of the stairwell. They seemed to go up as far as the top of the building. He took a deep breath and started to follow the others.

His fears were well justified, they climbed and climbed and climbed. Each floor they arrived at had several doors leading off to other parts of the complex, yet there was no respite. The group continued upward until they did eventually stop on the top floor. Ben looked out of a window to his right at a sight that took his breath away.

Stretching out as far as the eye could see, the dense green forests painted a picture of such beauty that Ben could not think of anywhere he had visited that could rival it. Oh the dramatic landscapes of the Lake District are astonishing but compared to this, they look more like a well kept garden.

The tree tops, deep green in colour, were so dense that it was only by studying them very closely he could see they were in fact multiply sign shaped. The various sizes of the trees gave the forest canopy a smooth undulating flow that looked like a green ocean whose waves had been stopped in time by taking a photograph.

Prime Number 2 opened a door on the left which led onto the roof of the building. The bright sunlight burst through the opening and a slight breeze touched the back of Ben's neck, causing him to turn around. There, beyond the opening, he could see six equilateral triangles perched upon triangular frames. Mounted underneath each of them was a single seat with a joystick type control to the front.

"I hope no one's afraid of heights?" 2 proclaimed as he walked onto the roof top.

Ben's eyes widened.

"We're going to fly!"

"Of course," said Pi, "how else do you think we were going to get there?"

Adder smiled at Ben.

"But I've never flown before," the shock of finding out the mode of transportation was clearly audible in Ben's voice, "I mean, I've been on a plane but never actually flown by myself."

"Don't worry," said Adder, trying to calm Ben's exasperated expression, "you'll be fine."

Ben followed Adder out into the open. The view from the window paled into insignificance compared to being exposed to the elements with a full 360o vista.

A number of blue triangles were busy doing jobs around the place, with a couple of them already strapping Prime Number 2 and Pi into their flying machines. Adder was the next to be escorted to his vessel, quickly followed by Ben. Two of the blue triangles hopped over, taking him by the hand and guided him over to one of the suspended flying triangles.

As he got closer, Ben could see that the triangular frame work was in fact a giant catapult. Two silver, tubular triangles joined together by a very thick, light brown rubber band. The flying triangle was supported by this elastic with one of the points facing in the direction of the cosine forest.

∞

Ben climbed into the seat under this wing. The blue triangles tightened his belts and tested the straps to ensure they were safe. Once convinced the young lad was firmly held in, one of them left to check on everyone else whilst the other told Ben how to control his craft.

"What what righty ho!" he said in a very posh accent, "This is your stick; you use it to guide your glider up, down, left and right. Left is left and right is right but forward is down and back is up, check?"

"Check what?" said Ben a little confused.

"No check as in check!"

The triangle gave Ben the thumbs up.

"Oh right, yes, check," said Ben holding his thumb skyward as well.

"Good job, good job, right have fun and tally ho!"

The triangle patted Ben on the knee then stepped back quickly. All of a sudden, Ben could feel himself being pulled back. The sound of the elastic stretching alarmed him. He looked over towards Adder; his craft was also being pulled back. For a moment they were stationary, then twang! Before Ben could think, he was thrown forward and was airborne.

Ben grabbed the joystick in sheer panic, pushing forward on it was he did. This caused him to suddenly see the tops of the trees whizzing past at a ferocious speed. Realising that the trees were now getting closer rather quickly, Ben reversed his action and pulled back. The glider swooped to face the sky, brushing Ben's feet on the highest of the leaves before heading straight up. Ben screamed with both fear and delight, it's like riding a rollercoaster at a theme park, he thought. The sky soon turned into the Great Hall upside-down followed shortly by the treetops, before the loop-the-loop completed with the sight of his companions flying off toward the mountain range.

He straightened the stick, which levelled off the glider and caught his breath. The aerial stunt had increased his acceleration so it wasn't long before he caught up with the others. By the time he reached them, the additional speed he acquired had reduced so instead of overtaking them, he ended up flying by their side.

The Hypotenuse Mountains grew in size as they got closer to them. Now Ben could understand why they had never been breached, the sheer size of them was almost too much to comprehend. 2 dipped his craft to increase speed and took the lead, everyone followed as he flew towards a ledge a good 5 metres over the treetops.

Like an expert, 2 landed on the ledge followed by Adder. Pi tried to make a touchdown, but got his approach speed wrong and had to pull up. Ben suddenly realised that not only had he never flown before but, more importantly at this time, he had never landed.

He wracked his brain, trying to remember how he did this on the flight simulator he played on his computer at home.

"Push down," he said to himself, "and just at the last moment, pull up slightly."

His landing was almost perfect, with just a little bounce. He removed his belts and jumped out of the glider with the biggest grin on his face.

"Waaaaahhhhh look out below!"

Ben jumped back and fell onto his bum, as Pi's flying triangle came hurtling across the ledge, before coming to an abrupt stop up against the wall of the mountainside.

Prime Number 2 went over to see is he was alright, Adder come over to check on Ben.

"Nice landing," he said, helping Ben to his feet.

"Thank you," said Ben rubbing his posterior, "how's Pi?"

The two looked over at the triangle propped up against the mountainside. There was the sound of a slight kafuffle, before 2 reappeared followed by Pi.

"It's alright," Pi exclaimed, holding one hand in the air, "I'm okay and the glider's fine as well."

Ben walked over to the edge and looked down, it's quite a drop, he thought.

"We landed up here so that we can get a good take off for our return."

Explained 2, "now, the path leading to the caves is over here."

2 walked over in the direction of Pi's clumsy landing. At the end of the ledge, a clear path leading down the side of the mountain was visible. The party of four began to descend and soon the light of the sun was hidden by the trees. The noise of the forest sounded more like a jungle with squeaks, warbles and woohars echoing from all directions. Ben tried to imagine what the creatures that would make such noises could look like, but found it hard to think of anything but maths symbols and numbers.

The path continued downwards until they reached the brown earth of the forest floor. About 2 metres in front of them, the huge opening of a cave led into the underbelly of the mountain they had just been on. With all the noises swilling around them, Ben feared that there might be a bear in there. "Don't worry," said Adder in response to this idea, "deep in this cave, is the door which is guarded by a platoon of ohms. If there were any bears here, they'd be gone by now."

The four of them entered the gloomy light of the cave, Pi, from somewhere Ben didn't see, produced a light sphere, like the ones Ben had seen in the catacombs of the Great Hall. It gave off enough light for them all to see where they were going.

As they walked deeper and deeper into the cave, the light from outside disappeared leaving them with only the sphere's illumination to show the way. Amongst the shadows, Ben noticed pictures drawn on the walls, pictures of numbers and letters and maths signs. To Ben they looked like equations, Adder assured him that the Scholars had investigated them thoroughly and reckoned they were drawn by prehistoric numbers.

"Something to do with the split between the Numbers and Letters in a time before records and way before the building of the city."

Ben still thought they looked like something he had see in one of his lessons, but not being very good at anything mathematical, he bowed to the knowledge of his very learned friend.

The party walked for about five minutes before they met their first ohm. As they came into sight, he jumped to attention, ready to follow any command given. Adder told him to 'stand down', and asked him to lead them to the door.

The ohm slammed his foot hard to the floor, causing an echo.

"Yes sir, General Sir, right away sir!"

The party followed the little horseshoe deeper into the mountain. Ben noticed more and more drawings on the walls, all following a similar theme to the previous ones. The further they walked, the more ohms they met each set standing to attention as their General passed by. After another ten minutes or so, the long corridor opened out into a room, lit on all sides by light spheres. Directly opposite the entrance, was the door, bright red and made of stone.

There was no furnishing to speak of, no handle, no hole for a key, no visible sign of any hinges, just a red painted slab of stone. The only reason you could tell it was a door of some kind, was the fact that it was slightly recessed from the rest of the wall.

Surrounding the door were more pictures of numbers and letters, intermingled with maths signs. To the left, carved into the rock, was what looked like keys on a computer keyboard, three rows of letters; only instead of them starting in the top left with the letter Q and spelling the word QWERTY as you read from left to right, it started with the letter A and continued alphabetically. Above this, was the puzzle Ben had solved back at the Vault.

Now he could see how old it was, written in the same faded paint used to draw the pictures, this isn't prehistoric, he thought. His mind was trying to figure out what was happening here. One thing Ben was sure of was that this wasn't going to be what everyone was expecting.

"I don't think this is a way to beat the Alphas," he whispered to Adder before making his way across the room to the keyboard.

Adder's eyebrows scrunched into the middle of his forehead as he contemplated what Ben had just said.

Closer to the keys, Ben could see how old these things were. Each key was a carved piece of rock set perfectly into the wall. On the face of each key, the letters had been scratched on, then painted over.

Ben started to type in the answer he had worked out. He placed his finger against the M and pressed, it took more force than he had anticipated but, with a little effort, he heard a click. After removing his finger he noticed that the key had remained depressed. Next was the A, then the T. Each key making a deep clicking noise which, Ben thought was also coming from the door. H. He moved his finger over the final letter, his nervousness showed through the shaking in his hand. He took a deep breath and pressed S.

A very loud bang came from the door and, dust burst out into the room from its edges. A grinding, scraping sound, like rock being rubbed against rock, filled the air. The floor, walls and ceiling of the cave began to shake and small pieces of rock fell around the waiting party.

Ben ran back over to Adder who, for the first time since Ben had known him, had an expression of uncertainty. Pi and 2 moved closer together and the Ohms, brave little souls that they are, manoeuvred themselves into a position between the party and the door.

Like beams of the sun bursting through a cloud, light spilled in through the dust. The door was opening. Fresh air rushed in, making the dust dance in swirls through the light. After a few seconds, the sound and the rumbling ceased. Everyone moved forward slightly, in anticipation of some kind of revelation.

From the light, a shadow moved towards them, it's shape, indefinable, due to the dust in the air and the light behind it.

"Oh my stars!" Exclaimed 2, as he realised what it was, "It's a trap!"

Standing in the doorway was a, dark red, capital letter A. The ohms moved forward to protect the dignitaries, Adder too, slid forward to help them. Pi and Prime Number 2 backed up towards the entrance of the cave. Suddenly, everything clicked into place in Ben's mind.

"WAIT!" he shouted, "it's not what you think!"

$1 \times 9 = 9$

$2 \times 9 = 18$

$3 \times 9 = 27$

$4 \times 9 = 36$

$5 \times 9 = 45$

$6 \times 9 = 54$

$7 \times 9 = 63$

$8 \times 9 = 72$

$9 \times 9 = 81$

$10 \times 9 = 90$

$E = MC2$

$A + B = C$

$A = 6$

$B = 4$

Chapter
9
nine

Chapter Nine

During all the rumbling, shaking and scraping, Ben had been trying to remember why the pictures on the walls looked so familiar. He cast his mind back to being at school, sitting in a lesson he wasn't that interested in, reconstructing it in his mind.

This served two purposes one; he didn't have to think about what was going on in the cave around him, and two; if he could only remember what these drawings reminded him of, he could figure out what was actually going on around him.

He imagined being sat in a Physics class about two or three months ago. Mr Hawkon, their Physics tutor was waffling on about the laws of how things moved and how gravity worked and other stuff that just didn't capture Ben's imagination.

He tried to pay more attention this time round, replaying every detail of the lesson.

"And that's when Albert Einstein came up with this."

Mr Hawkon wrote some letters on the blackboard, E=MC2.

"This," he said, "is the theory of relativity. Energy equals matter times the speed of light squared."

But it wasn't this theory that Ben was now interested in, it was the letters, or to be more precise, the mathematics done with letters.

He moved from one class room to another, now he was in maths with Mrs Peacock. She was writing on the blackboard, A+B=C, at the same time she was telling the class the question she wanted them to answer.

"If A equals six, and B equals four what does C equal?"

She turned to the blank faces in the room; Ben put his hand up to ask a question.

"Yes Ben." She said, allowing him to speak.

"What do you mean Miss?"

Mrs Peacock explained again what this lesson was all about. It was at this moment that Ben shouted "Wait!"

∞

Now, fully aware of everything that was going on in the cave, Ben pushed his way forward past Adder and the ohms, positioning himself between them and the letter A.

"This is not an alpha and it's not a trap!"

He turned to look at the letter, who hadn't said a word during all of this.

"This," he said beginning to smile, "is Algebra."

Adder slithered his way past the troops.

"What do you mean Ben?"

"It's mathematics but, done with letters."

"Don't be foolish!" exclaimed 2, from the back of the cave, "you can't do sums with letters, it's a trap I tell you!"

"NO!" shouted Ben, "Algebra is where letters and numbers meet. The letters represent numbers in a sum. The maths is always the same only the numbers change."

"He's right you know," the soft voice of the Algebra came forth from behind Ben, "My people are the link between numbers and letters."

The silence that fell across the room was broken by Pi. He shuffled forward so that he could get a better position to be heard from.

"You mean you represent a number?" he began, "Like I do?"

"Yes Pi," said the A, "only the number you represent is a constant, you never change."

"But Ray Dias and Dye Ameter, they change?"

"In my world," the A puffed out his chest with pride, "we call them R and D."

Ben understood more and more, his mind raced with various mathematical questions to try and find one that would suit this situation and let everybody understand what he did. Just like Adder had been doing with him all through the city. Ben realised that's what Adder was trying to do, make him understand how it all worked. Then he remembered Mrs Peacock again.

"A plus B equals C." He began, "If A equals six, and B equals four what does C equal?"

"What a stupid question!" Proclaimed 2.

"Ten," said Adder.

Ben smiled.

Adder continued to explain his answer, "Six plus four equals ten. So if A is six and B is four then C must be ten."

"So if letters can be numbers and numbers can be letters," Prime Number 2 said moving forward, "why do the Alphas want to attack us?"

"The Alphas are attacking you?" asked the A, with a great deal of surprise, "that's not what's supposed to happen."

The dark red A moved forward towards the exit that led back to the forest.

"We have no time to lose, I must talk to them."

Ben took a look out of the door onto the land of Algebra. A beautiful meadow stretched out to the horizon with pink and blue flowers dotted around amongst the lush green grass. Adder moved over to Ben and placed his tail on his shoulder.

"Well done Ben," said the serpent, "I knew you had it in you."

Ben turned round and smiled, it felt good to be complimented, especially when it something to do with maths. Adder told the Ohms to keep watch before the two friends left.

A, 2 and Pi had made good pace up the cave and were two thirds back to the entrance by the time Ben and Adder had caught up with them. The Prime Number and Pi were trying to explain what had been going on back at the city with the pending attack. All A could say was "This isn't how it's supposed to be."

The five of them returned to the noise of the forest before climbing the steep path back to the landing site. Ben felt different in himself, like he had found something that he didn't know was missing, but was quite obviously absent once discovered. He thought of all the arguments he'd had with his mother and stepfather realising that, if he'd just stopped to think about things, all the misunderstandings could been avoided.

A little bit out of breath, the party, now with an extra member, arrived back at their transport. Two things suddenly dawned on Ben, one; there was now five of them and only four flying triangles and two; they now had to take off again by dropping off the edge of a cliff. Neither of these two scenarios had entered his mind before now, so the time for thinking was seriously reduced.

The fact that Ben was the first to realise the numbers problem, combined with the lack of thinking time, caused him to say something he really didn't want to.

"Algebra A can fly back with me."

As the words left his lips, he knew that he wasn't the best pilot to take on the task, a fact lost on everyone else as they agreed.

2 was the first to leave, dragging his craft to the edge, strapping himself in then, with a joyful shout, pushing his blue triangle off the side. The glider fell for about half a metre before swooping back up into the air.

Pi was next, this time Adder and Ben helped by making sure the straps were tight then pushing the hapless leader of the round circle off the cliff. As with 2, Pi's flying machine dropped about the same distance before catching the air under its wing and soaring up high into the sky.

Adder suggested that Ben and A should go next, that way he could help them take off. This seemed like a good idea so they dragged his glider over to the edge and told A to climb up. Once in the seat, Ben sat on A's lap. The seat belts had to be loosened from the first trip due to the extra size now in the seat. Adder checked the straps and gave Ben the thumbs up.

"Check," said Ben returning the gesture.

"I hope you know how to fly this thing?" was the question from the squashed letter.

"Don't worry," Ben said, trying not to sound nervous, "I've already done this once today."

Adder started his count down, "Three, Two, One..."

Ben wasn't sure what the last word Adder said was, his mind fully on the fact that he, and the letter behind him, were now heading towards the forest at a very alarming rate. Ben thought, whilst trying to pull back on the joystick, that in about half a metre, the air would catch under the wing and they would be flying back to the city. What he hadn't considered, or anyone else for that matter, was the extra weight of the letter crushed in behind him.

The glider was rapidly heading downwards and the trees were getting closer. Ben gritted his teeth, closed his eyes and, putting all his strength into it, pulled back on the joystick as hard as he could. The stick moved towards him and, with the leaves of the treetops bushing his feet for the second time today, the glider swooped back up. Ben quickly levelled the stick which in turn controlled the triangle and resumed normal flight.

"Wow! That was exciting." Said A.

Ben just took a deep breath, you're the lucky one, he thought, you couldn't see the trees coming.

After a few minutes, the Great Hall of Mathamagical came into view. From this angle, the building seemed even more impressive than it did from the front. Ben could see the first two gliders in front of them, which made him think about Adder, had he taken off alright?

Ben looked round to his left, nothing, then to his right. There, flying just behind them, was Adder. Ben gave a little wave to acknowledge his friend, Adder returned the compliment.

After a short time, Ben could see the first two approaching the landing pad. 2 was first with what seemed, from this distance, like another perfect landing. Pi, on the other hand, seemed to hit the roof of the building with great speed, and very quickly disappeared out of view.

Ben guided his craft in towards the roof, using the same tactic he had before, push forward then back a little and unlike, the take off from the mountain, he allowed for the extra weight.

Like someone who had been flying all their life, he touched the glider down without even a bounce this time. The little blue triangles came running over to help the lad out of the machine. On the other side of the roof, Ben saw Pi's glider propped up against the wall of the stairwell. Pi was surrounded by blue triangles; he assured them that he was quite all right in his usual manner.

∞

As Ben hopped out of his seat Algebra A stretched. The sight of the letter made the triangles panic.

"It's alright, he's with us!" Shouted 2.

Adder's glider landed perfectly and the snake was out and coming over to the rest of the party before any of the flight staff could get to him. The triangles were still a bit wary of the letter but, being as there was no time to explain, the five had to leave them wondering what was going on.

The stairs were much easier on the way back down; though it was still tiring due to the speed they were all moving at. By the time they got to the bottom, even Adder was panting. They went through the door and out into the Great Hallway. There, by the entrance to the building, with the sunlight behind him, was The 1.

Prime Number 2 dashed up the corridor to greet his leader but, before he could get there, The 1 spoke.

"What is this?" he boomed, "An Alpha in the Great Hall!"

"No sir!" shouted 2 still running, "we will explain on the way."

"To where?"

"The main gates!"

2 carried on, past the Crystal Leader of Numbers and out into the daylight. Adder, Ben, Pi and A, hurried towards the front door. The 1 was looking both perplexed and displeased at the same time. It's a look that only people in authority can really get right. Pi was the first to reach the door. He pushed and held it open for the others. First the dark red A then Adder went through, Ben stopped by The 1.

"Please sir, you must come with us?"

The head digit looked down at Ben. he could see from his face that this young human had something very important to say, with very little time to say it.

"No Ben," said Pi from the door, "The 1 never leaves the Great Hall."

Ben looked up at The 1, "Please sir?"

Without saying a word, The 1 did something he had never done before and walked through the doors of the Great Hall, out into the day.

At the end of the avenue of shapes, 2 had already summoned the long white minus sign. He opened the back door so that the others could enter first. Algebra A climbed in, Adder stopped and turned back to see where Ben was. Adder and 2 couldn't believe what they saw, flanked by Pi and Ben The 1 was walking down the grey path towards them. Adder bowed his head as the glass number got into the back of the transport.

After the snake, Pi and Ben were safely in, 2 joined them slamming the door shut behind them.

"To the main gate," commanded 1.

The driver, a yellow number 6, set off at full speed. The force of the acceleration pushed all the passengers to the very back of the vehicle. Such was the speed that, every corner the minus sign car went round, threw the party from the left to the right and back to the left again. After a couple of very bumpy minutes, the driver hit the brakes and the passengers were once again at the front of the compartment.

1 was not amused, he grunted and snorted before making various remarks involving the driver, how we won't be working for him again and this was the reason he never left the Great Hall. With all the throwing about, Ben and the others never got a chance to tell The 1 about anything that had transpired previously.

They opened the door to see an army of Ohms running every which way they could around the main gate.

"The Alphas have reached the gate!" was the cry that could be heard from several directions.

Algebra A turned to The 1.

"It's time I got you and the leader of the Alphas together."

The dark red A left the vehicle followed closely by The 1. Silently, 2, Pi, Adder and Ben exited into the madness that was going on around them. The Crystal 1 took the lead and walked towards the gates. He gestured to some ohms standing to the right, next to a series of chains and cogs. The Ohms jumped into action, turning wheels and pulling chains.

The cogs began to turn with loud, teeth clenching, grinding sounds, could do with a bit of oil, thought Ben. More grinding mixed with rattling chains then, a sudden thud and click. The gates began to open. Ben and Adder moved up behind the leader of numbers.

Through the gap in the gate, Ben could see what everyone around here was panicking about. All across the positive lands to the right and the negative lands of the left, were letters. Upper and lower case, thousands of them, from A through to Z, every conceivable member of the alphabet was there, in force, yelling and jeering.

1 motioned to the Ohms to stop working the mechanism which they did immediately.   Ben looked round to see where 2 and Pi were. The two of them had stayed back by the minus sign; Ben waved his hand to beckon them forward. Both dignitaries declined with a shake of, what could only be considered to be, their heads. Ben turned back to the situation in front of him.

The 1 and Algebra A were walking through the opening to face the letter army. Adder turned to Ben.

"I think your job is done here," he said in a very stern way, "You should wait with Pi and Prime Number 2."

"No Way!" protested Ben, "I haven't come this far, worked out all these things and learnt this much to not know what's going on."

"It could be dangerous?"

"I'm coming with you."

Adder's expression of concern changed to one of pride. This young boy who had seemed so lost in this new world had grown in confidence and was now being as brave as Adder had known he could be. The snake nodded his head with respect before turning to join his leader and the A.

Ben took a deep breath. He hadn't thought it through, just acted upon his instincts. He knew that there was something more for him to do here and he wasn't about to let what was obviously a misunderstanding, ruin everything he had just achieved. Raising his head up and for the first time ever, fully believing in himself, Ben walked through the open gates.

The noise of the army turned to an eerie silence as the four emerged in front of them. The sight of so many angry letters filled Ben full of dread, making him want to run away. He clenched his fists and, unlike before when he was back at home, resisted the temptation to leave.

"I'm here to see your leader, Capitol Z." Shouted 1.

"They've captured one of ours?" came a shout from the crowd, obviously just spotting the Algebra letter.

This call started the jeering again, a noise so loud, Ben could hardly hear himself think let alone what the dark red A was trying to say to calm them all down. Directly opposite where the four were standing, the crowd began to move, parting to make way for their leader. Out of the maddening letters, a Z, looking as though it was made of ruby, emerged. The army fell silent once more.

"Are you here to surrender 1?" The Z asked with a respectful tone.

"I am here to sort out this mess." 1 replied.

"Have they been treating you well my Alpha brother?" Z said to the Algebra A. Wearing a disapproving look the A responded, "I am not an Alpha."

The shock of this statement was audible amongst the Alpha troops. Z looked confused and turned his attention back to 1.

"Is this some kind of brain washing?"

"No." replied 1, "this A has information that can bring an end to these hostilities."

Ben was becoming frustrated by all these macho games. It was obvious that the leader of the numbers or the commanding letter were neither trusting, nor believing each other.

The letter leader was so convinced that the dark red A was one of his kind, that had somehow been programmed to say whatever the numbers wanted him to say, that whatever information the A did give would be considered a lie. The letters had already made up their minds and nothing the Algebra could do would change that.

∞

Ben understood how unfair this whole thing was. He knew it was up to him to stop this nonsense.

"Why are you here?" he suddenly asked.

The Z looked over at Ben, giving him such a stare that Ben felt humbled. He shook off his feeling of belittlement and spoke again, with a much more determined voice.

"Why are you here?"

"Because we know what the numbers have planned." Said the Z, "We know they want to change all the letters into numbers."

"And how do you know this?"

Adder looked at Ben, unsure of where the young lad was going with this line of questioning.

"It is written in the old scriptures found on the walls of a cave at the foot of the Anagram Mountains." The ruby Z proclaimed, "The pictorials show letters turning into numbers."

Ben had been thinking about something the Algebra A had said, 'it isn't supposed to be like this.'

"And at the end of this cave," Ben chose his words very carefully, "is there a door with a keypad next to it?"

Again an audible surprise could be heard from the Alphas.

"Yes" answered the Z.

"And above this keypad is there a riddle written?"

Z looked at Ben with suspicion, "yes, a number problem."

Interesting, thought Ben.

"I have just solved an English problem on a similar door in a similar cave," explained Ben, "with very similar drawings on the walls, only here, the mountains are called the Hypotenuse Mountains and the numbers thought the drawing meant nothing."

Ben moved up next to the dark red A.

"The door leads to the land of Algebra and this letter," Ben gestured to the A, "came through that door."

"We set up the caves many years before the cities were built." Said A, "It was supposed to stop the fighting, not encourage it."

Both the Crystal 1 and the Ruby Z looked at the Algebra letter. The A began to tell the story.

"Before the cities, all three of our people lived together only the Numerics and the Alphas were always arguing about who was more important.

The Algebras thought that if they went off and hid, both of your people would come looking for us, help each other with the search.

We set up the doors with a Maths problem on the Alphas side and an English problem on the Numbers. The idea was, that whomever found them first would ask for the others to help solve the problem, thus working together."

The A looked down at the floor.

"Only it doesn't seem to have gone to plan," the Algebras voice began to crack slightly, as if he was upset, "you didn't seem to miss us. From what I can see you were more interested in not getting on, than working together."

Ben felt sorry for the letter that is also a number. He had figured out that the Algebras had set up the whole door and riddle thing, but he had no idea, until now, why?

"You should be ashamed of yourselves," he said as if he was telling off a small child, "Letters and Numbers are equally important. Without either of them I wouldn't be able to read a book or tell what time the next train was going to be."

Ben explained to the two leaders what Algebra was, how you can use letters to represent numbers. He also told them that you could write messages in numbers, as a code. The numbers would represent letters so you could decipher the message when you knew which number was which letter.

"I'm sorry." Said the Z to the Algebra A.

"So am I." said The 1.

Adder smiled more broadly than he had ever smiled before. Ben had not only solved the riddle he was brought here to do, but had also realised how

∞

both sides had misunderstood what they were supposed to do.

"I think," said the General, "this calls for a celebration. A party to welcome back the Algebras and cement the friendship that the Alphas and Numerics should have had all these years."

Algebra A, The 1 and Capital Z agreed.

Z turned to his people, "There will be no war!" He shouted, "Tonight, there will be a party!"

The cheer from the troops was emulated moments later when the leader of the numbers conveyed the same message to citizens of Mathamagical.

1x10=10

2x10=20

3x10=30

4x10=40

5x10=50

6x10=60

7x10=70

8x10=80

9x10=90

10x10=100

Chapter
10
ten

Chapter Ten

Messages were sent back to Alphabetown and to the Algebra lands, summoning everyone to Mathamagical. Soon the city was full of numbers and letters from all races. The Alphas were slightly taller than the Algebras and their colours were different too. The Algebras were coloured more like the Numerics, bold prime colours, whereas the Alphas were softer pastel shades. This stopped any confusion as to who came from where.

As night fell, the merriment intensified with dancing and laughter on every street. Bands made up of all races played music that filled the air, children played games and the hosts brought food and drinks out for everyone to enjoy.

The atmosphere was like nothing Ben had ever experienced before and, even though all around him happiness prevailed, he felt ever so slightly sad. Adder noticed Ben's melancholy and asked what the matter was.

"I've got to go home soon," said Ben tucking into a sandwich, "I have my own misunderstanding to sort out."

"I know," comforted Adder, "and now I think you'll be able to."

Ben smiled, he had learned a lot on his adventure and not just how to fly or the new understanding he had in mathematics. He had learned how strong he could be in himself, how confident he could be with his own abilities and how, despite everything else, not everything is as it first seems.

"Adder," he said, taking a drink of pop, "why are you still a snake?"

Adder smiled. "That's a story for another day."

The two sat in silence watching the festivities and enjoyed the time they had left. From the stadium, a white ball of light shot high into the night's sky with a whiz, then BANG! The city lit up in multiple colours. More and more impressive explosions filled the sky as the fireworks display, organised by the Round Circle, impressively celebrated the new union.

The pyrotechnics lasted about half an hour after which Ben and Adder walked round to Pi's house. They moved through the crowded streets, down Tangent Avenue and back to the bright Purple building with the green door.

∞

3.141593, a number Ben wouldn't forget in a hurry.

They rang the bell and waited, this time Ben didn't lean on the door. After a short while, Pi arrived at the entrance with Dye Ameter, Ray Dius and Sir Cumferance.

"Ah good, you're here." said Pi, letting the others out before closing and locking the door behind him, "Did you see the fireworks?"

"Yes," said Ben with a smile, "they were very good."

"We were just about to come looking for you two," said Ray, "we all have to go to the main square to meet up with the Prime Numbers."

The main square is about two blocks east from the stadium. On Thursdays it is used for a market, selling everything from fruit and vegetables to pots and pans. Most of the time, it's just a place where the folks of Mathamagical eat their lunch when the weather was nice, today it was being used for the official welcoming ceremony for the Algebras.

Z and 1 agreed that, being as they were holding the celebrations in the city, that they should welcome back the Algebras here as well. This was the first joint decision made by the new alliance.

A very long table was set up down one side of the square, in the middle sat the main leaders. On the left sat 1 with Z on the right, between them was Algebra A. The Prime Numbers, Vowels and Algebra dignitaries sat, in no particular order, on either side of them.

The square was beginning to fill with numbers and letters wishing to witness this historic event. Ben looked at the size of the area, you'll have to be lucky to see this, he thought, as to him there definitely wasn't enough room for everyone.

Ben and Adder walked with the members of the Round Circle over to the table. Pi, Ray, Dye and Sir Cumferance took their places.

"Ben," said Prime Number 2, "you can sit here, next to me."

He gestured to the empty chair on his right. Ben smiled, looked at Adder then back at 2.

"I'm sorry sir, but I won't be joining you for the ceremony."

∞

Everyone at the table looked over at him. Not for the first time, Ben felt uncomfortable about this.

"This is your day," the young lad said with a maturity beyond his years, "you should enjoy it."

"But Ben," said Algebra A, "this wouldn't be happening if it wasn't for you."

"Thank you but," Ben paused, a feeling of sadness welling up inside of him, "I need to go home."

He hated saying good bye, he always felt like crying when his Gran went home after a two week stay.

"Don't be silly," she'd say, seeing the sombre look on his face, "you'll see me again soon enough."

This time, Ben felt like he was saying goodbye for a much longer period of time. He couldn't imagine ever coming back here, no matter how much he wanted to. 1 stood up from his seat.

"I will speak for the entire land of Mathamagical," he said, booming his words out so that everyone in the square could hear, "Ben, we owe you a debt of gratitude and, should you ever need us, we the people of Mathamagical will be here for you."

Capital Z then rose.

"I concur with my new friend," he said, also in a very loud voice, "you have taught us much and the Alphas will never forget that."

Algebra A was the next to rise. He looked at Ben and smiled.

"Even though it was not planned this way, I'm glad you were the one to solve the puzzle. I hope to see you again soon."

Ben thanked them all for their kindness. Just then, a voice came from behind him that he recognised.

"You better had come back soon," said the teacher from the school, "you promised the children some stories."

He turned to see the brown number 9; she was wearing her bright red rimmed party glasses. Ben smiled and promised he would be back. She gave him a big hug and wished him well.

Ben said his goodbyes to everyone at the table that he knew, and then turned to leave. Adder started to walk with him.

"You stay and enjoy this moment." Ben said to the snake.

"Believe me Ben," Adder said, out the side of his mouth so no one else would notice, "I'd rather come with you."

Ben laughed then continued to exit the square. From behind him, he could hear a single loud slow clap. He turned back to see where the sound was coming from. The Crystal 1, leader of all numbers was applauding. Z followed suit and soon the whole square was giving Ben a heartfelt round of applause. Ben had never felt so proud in all his life. He waved at everyone he could, then, wiping a tear from his eye, he left.

The two didn't say much as they trundled back through the streets towards the gates. The conversation didn't pick up much once they were on the zero path. In fact, nothing was said at all until they reached the spot where Adder first brought Ben into this world.

"Here," said Adder, "I want you to have this."

He handed Ben a small, gold infinity sign badge.

"Thank you," said Ben.

"No, thank you," replied Adder, "now you remember the spell to make you small? Just reverse it to make yourself big again."

Adder swished his tail in the air, the end began to glow and he continued to move it back and forth, faster and faster until, like a sparkler on bonfire night, Ben could see that Adder was drawing an infinity sign. The symbol grew brighter and brighter, growing bigger and bigger. In the middle of the light, Ben could see his science classroom. He looked at Adder, then back down the path. Clutching the gold badge tight in his hand he drew a deep breath.

"See you later Adder!"

He jumped into the light. The sound around him changed from outside, wide open space to enclosed no air movement. This sudden change took a few seconds to get used to. He looked back only to see skirting board.

The room was huge; he was, after all, still a tenth of his original size. Sunlight was now invading the classroom, and even though the storm had long passed, the wreckage from Old Invincible's failed attempt to stay upright was still very much in evidence.

By the looks of things, Ben had only been away for the night. He racked his brain to remember the Mathamagical spell that would make him bigger again.

"1 to 10, 10 to 1, Scale up Ben Small to this ratio."

No sooner had he said the words than everything in the room began to change in size and started becoming smaller. Or that's how it seemed to Ben, in fact, he was getting bigger. The one thing he forgot to account for was that he was standing under one of the benches. His rapidly increasing size caused him to bump his head again.

"How many times am I going to do that," he said to himself, whilst rubbing the area that had just collided with the underside of the worktop.

He scrambled over to his bag, packed away his torch, which was lying on the floor giving out a dim light and left. I have to get home before anyone notices I'm gone, he thought.

He flung open the door and ran down the corridor. The sounds of his feet hitting the polished floor echoed through the empty school. He was running so fast that every corner he had to navigate caused him to nearly fall. Right, left, rightdown the stairs, onto the main corridor.

Stood by the main doors was Mr Crossmon, the caretaker. He looked up with a mixture of surprise and annoyance to see Ben running towards him.

"Oi you, stop right there." He shouted.

But Ben wasn't about to stop for anybody. He put his head down and gave that little bit extra. Mr Crossmon dodged this way and that, to try and stop the intruder, but Ben was too agile. Just at the last moment, he dropped to his knees and slid on the shiny, polished floor right through the caretakers legs.

Now on the other side of this human obstacle, Ben was clear to make good his escape. He burst through the doors, out of the school gates and up the road. All he had to do, was get back into his bedroom before anyone noticed he

∞

was gone.

Turning the corner onto Lightridge Avenue, Ben saw that his plan wasn't going to work. Outside his house there were two police cars parked. Ben's mother was standing in the front garden crying, a woman police officer was trying her best to give some kind of comfort.

Ben slowed his run to a walk, he felt sick. He didn't like seeing his mother cry and he knew that she was crying because of him. Just then, his step-dad Stephen shouted something. Everyone, his mother, the police and the neighbours that had come out to gawp turned to look at him, again Ben felt uncomfortable.

Stephen and his mother came running up the street to him. Ben was prepared for the worst, but instead of being shouted at and told he was grounded, his mother grabbed hold of him and swept him off the floor into her arms, giving him the biggest hug he could remember.

Stephen kept asking him if he was alright and 'where have you been?' and 'we've been so worried'. His mother eventually let go and was content to just hold his hand. Ben, now in floods of tears, explained why he ran away and, how the fact that they had not believed him had made him angry.

Stephen and his mother apologised for being so judgemental. They all walked back to the house. As they got to the gate, his parents stopped to talk to the police. Ben put his hand in his pocket, he felt something hard. He pulled it out, the infinity badge Adder had given him. Now, in daylight, Ben could see how beautiful it was. He put it back in his pocket.

His attention was taken away from the conversation the police woman was having with his mother by a hissing noise coming from the bushes by the front garden wall. He turned in the direction of the sound, up onto the wall slid Adder. Ben smiled at the snake. The snake smiled back, winked his right eye then, with a swish of his tail, left. The boy sighed; he felt a slight sorrow at the parting of his scaly friend and wondered if they would ever meet again.

Ben, his mother and his stepfather all thanked the police before going back into their house for a nice breakfast and a long chat.

Look out for Ben and Adder in their next adventure

ANAGRAMAPHOBIA

CPSIA information can be obtained
at www.ICGtesting.com
Printed in the USA
LVHW080806080521
686864LV00020B/680